Clyde Fitch

Nathan Hale

A Play in Four Acts

Clyde Fitch

Nathan Hale
A Play in Four Acts

ISBN/EAN: 9783743388840

Manufactured in Europe, USA, Canada, Australia, Japa

Cover: Foto ©Andreas Hilbeck / pixelio.de

Manufactured and distributed by brebook publishing software
(www.brebook.com)

Clyde Fitch

Nathan Hale

NATHAN HALE

A Play

In Four Acts

By
Clyde Fitch

New York
R. H. Russell, Mdcccxcix

Nathan Hale

Act First
April, 1775
The Union Grammar Schoolhouse in New London, Connecticut.

Act Second
September, 1776
At Colonel Knowlton's House, Harlem Heights.

Act Third
September, 1776
The First Scene: The Tavern of the Widow Chichester, Long Island.

The Second Scene: Outside the Tavern, early the next morning.

Act Fourth
The Next Night
The First Scene: The Tent of a British Officer.

The Second Scene: The Orchard on Colonel Rutger's Farm (now Pike and Monroe Streets, New York).

Act the First

Act the First

THE *Union Grammar Schoolhouse, New London, Connecticut, in* 1775. *It is a simple room with a door on the left side. At the back are two smallish windows through which are seen trees and the blue sky; between them is a big blackboard. At the right of the room is a small, slightly raised platform on which is the teacher's desk; on the latter are papers, quill pens, an old ink-well, pamphlets, and books. A large globe of the world stands beside the platform. On the wall behind hangs a " birch." In front of the platform, and to one side, is a three-legged dunce's stool, unoccupied for the present. Two long, low benches for the classes are placed beneath the blackboard, and the desks and benches for the scholars are placed on the left, facing the teacher's platform. It is toward noon of a sunny day, and the music of " Yankee Doodle " is in the air. As the curtain rises a very badly drawn, absurd picture is seen on the blackboard, representing the boys on the ice pond of Boston Common, with their thumbs to their noses, driving away the British army !* Alice Adams *is by the blackboard finishing this drawing.* Miss Adams *is one of the older pupils, somewhat of a hoyden, already a little of a woman, lovely to look upon, and altogether a charming, natural girl full of high spirits. All the scholars are half out of their places and they are laughing, shouting, talking, and gesticulating. Above the din, a* Boy's *voice is heard.*

TALBOT BOY.

IN *warning.*] Quick, Alice ! Teacher !

There is a wild scramble for their places, and just as Lebanon *enters sudden silence reigns. All pretend to be absorbed in their books, but keep one eye on* Lebanon *and the blackboard, till he, following their glances, discovers the drawing.*

[1]

LEBANON.

[*A prim and youthful assistant teacher, with a pompous manner, intended to deceive his pupils.*] Who drew that picture? [*There is silence.*] Who drew this picture? [*No one replies, and only a few suppressed giggles are heard.*] I will keep you all after hours till the boy confesses.

ALICE.

[*Interrupts mischievously.*] Perhaps it was a *girl*, sir. [*The children giggle and snicker.*]

LEBANON.

No interruptions! I will keep you all in till the boy confesses. [Lebanon *looks about expectantly; nobody speaks.*] I am in earnest.

TALBOT BOY.

It wasn't a boy, it was Alice Adams. [*The scholars hiss and cry "Shame! Shame!"*]

LEBANON.

Miss Alice Adams, stand up. [Alice *rises.*] Is that true?

ALICE.

[*Biting her lips to keep from laughing.*] Yes, sir.

LEBANON.

[*To* Alice.] Sit down. [*She does so, very leisurely.—To the Boy.*] Well, Master Talbot, you deserve to be punished more than Miss Adams, for telling on a fellow pupil, and on a girl, too. I shall report you both to Mr. Hale.

TOM ADAMS (*Alice's younger brother*).

Please tell him I did it, sir, instead of my sister. Mr. Hale's always punishing Alice.

ALICE.

No, Mr. Lebanon, that wouldn't be fair, sir. Besides, I want Mr. Hale to know how well I can draw. [*Smiling mischievously. All the scholars laugh.*]

LEBANON.

[*Raps on the table.*] Silence! That is enough. We will now begin the session in the usual manner by singing "God Save the King."

Act First

[*A knock on the door. All the scholars are excited and curious.*] Master Adams, please open the door. [Tom *goes to the door and opens it; all the children looking over the tops of their books curiously.*] Everybody's eyes on their books. [*Each one holds his book up before his face between him or her and* Lebanon.]

Mrs. Knowlton *and* Angelica *enter. Mrs.* Knowlton *is a handsome, but rather voluble and nervous lady, an undeterminated trifle past middle age. Her daughter,* Angelica, *is a pretty, quaint little creature, with a sentimental bearing; she is dressed in the top of the fashion.* Lebanon *rises and* Tom *returns to his place.*

ALICE.
[*Half rising in surprise, and sitting again immediately.*] Well! Angelica Knowlton! What are you doing here?

LEBANON.
[*Raps on his desk with his ruler.*] Miss Adams! [Angelica *throws* Alice *a kiss.*]

MRS. KNOWLTON.
Is this Mr. Hale?
[Alice *gives a little explosion of laughter, which is at once followed by giggles from all the children.* Lebanon *raps again sharply.*]

LEBANON.
No, madam, I am Mr. Lebanon, Mr. Hale's assistant.
[Alice *coughs very importantly.*]

MRS. KNOWLTON.
I wrote Mr. Hale I would visit his schoolhouse to-day with my daughter, Angelica, to arrange for her becoming a pupil. [*Bringing* Angelica *slightly forward with one hand;* Angelica *is embarrassed, and plays nervously with her parasol.*] Her cousin, Miss Adams, is already a scholar, and it will be well for the girls to be together. Angelica, dear, stop fiddling with your parasol, you make my nerves quite jumpy!

LEBANON.
Mr. Hale will be here in one moment, madam. Won't you be seated, meanwhile?

[3]

Nathan Hale

MRS. KNOWLTON.

Thank you, yes. Be careful of your dress, when you sit, Angelica—don't make any more creases than are absolutely necessary. [*They sit carefully in chairs placed for them by* Lebanon *beside the desk.*]

LEBANON.

Your daughter is a most intelligent appearing young lady, madam. I look forward with pleasure to instructing her.

MRS. KNOWLTON.

Thank you, sir, but it's only fair to tell you her appearances are deceitful. She is painfully backward in everything but spelling, and her spelling's a disgrace to the family. Angelica, dear, untie your bonnet strings; you'll get a double chin in no time if you're not more careful!

[Alice Adams *lifts her hand.*]

LEBANON.

What is it, Miss Adams?

ALICE.

Please may I go and kiss my aunt and cousin how d' you do? [*The scholars giggle softly.*]

MRS. KNOWLTON.

That will not be at all necessary, Mr. Lebanon.

LEBANON.

You must wait until recess, Miss Adams. Now, attention, please! [*The scholars all shut their books, which they have made a pretence of studying, and rise without noise.*]

MRS. KNOWLTON.

[*To* Angelica.] Do you like this teacher, my darling?

ANGELICA.

I think he is beautiful, mother.

MRS. KNOWLTON.

Well, that is scarcely the adjective I should use; *harmless* would be better I think. Cross your feet, my dear, it looks much more ladylike.

[4]

Act First

LEBANON.

[*Rising.*] Ready! [*He strikes a tuning fork on the desk, motions three times with his finger, and at the third stroke all begin to sing* " *God Save the King.*" Mrs. Knowlton *and* Angelica *rise and sing. All sing except* Tom Adams. *After the first line,* Lebanon *stops them.*] Stop! Thomas Adams is not singing. Now, *everyone*, mind, and Thomas, if you don't sing, it will be five raps on the knuckles. [*All sing except* Tom, *two lines;* Lebanon *again stops them.*] Thomas Adams, come forward! [Tom *comes slowly forward.*] I am ashamed of you, being disobedient in this manner, before your esteemed relative, too. What do you mean, sir?

TOM.

I won't sing " God Save the King."

LEBANON.

And why not?

TOM.

Because I hate him and his red coats. Hip! Hip! I say, for the Boston Indians, and Hooray for their tea-party! [*There is a low suppressed murmur of approval from the scholars, and a loud* "Oh!" *of astonishment from* Angelica.]

LEBANON.

We'll see if we can't *make* you sing. Hold out your hand. [Tom *holds out his hand, and* Lebanon *takes up his ruler.*]

ANGELICA.

Oh — [*She cries out and rises involuntarily.*] Oh, please, Mr. Teacher —

LEBANON.

[*After a moment's hesitation.*] I cannot be deaf to the voice of beauty. [*Bowing to* Angelica, *he lays down the ruler.*]

MRS. KNOWLTON.

Child, compose your nerves; watch your mother!

TOM.

Oh, you can whack me if you want. But when Mr. Hale's here, he don't punish me for not singing.

[5]

LEBANON.

He doesn't? How's that?

TOM.

No, sir. He said he didn't blame me!

LEBANON.

Mr. Hale said that?

TOM.

Yes, sir, and he said he had half a mind not to sing it himself any longer.

LEBANON.

That's treason! We'll see about that when Mr. Hale arrives. [Tom *goes back to his seat.*]

MRS. KNOWLTON.

Does Mr. Hale never come to the schoolhouse till toward noon?—Angelica! [*She motions aside to* Angelica *to pull down her skirts, — that her ankles are showing.*]

LEBANON.

No, madam. Only there was a rumor to-day that there had been bloodshed between the British and Americans at Concord, and Mr. Hale is at the Post waiting for news.

THE TALBOT BOY.

[*With his eyes turned toward one of the windows.*] Please, sir, here comes Mr. Hale now.

LEBANON.

Very well. You will all please begin again and sing, whether Master Adams sings or not.

TOM.

[*Who has been straining to see out.*] Mr. Hale is out of breath, and he's wondrous excited!

[Lebanon *raps for them to sing, and strikes tuning fork. The children sing—all except* Tom—*through three lines, when* Hale *enters, excited.*]

HALE.

[*Lifting his hand.*] Stop that singing! [*The children stop.*]

[6]

Act First

LEBANON.

Why is that, Mr. Hale?

HALE.

I won't have my school sing any more anthems to that tyrant!

LEBANON.

We will be punished for treason. Will you kindly notice the drawing on the board?

HALE.

Hello! Hello! [*Laughing.*] What is it?

THE JEFFERSON BOY.

It's our boys, sir, in Boston, driving the red coats off the Common.

LEBANON.

I have left the punishment for *you* to fix on, sir.

HALE.

Punishment! Punishment! Not a bit of it! Give the boy who did it a prize. Listen to me, boys and girls — how many of you are Whigs? Say "Aye." [*All but the* Talbot Boy *raise their right hands and shout "Aye!"*] Who's a Tory?

TALBOT BOY.

Aye! [*Raising his right hand, but he takes it down quickly as all the others hiss him.*]

HALE.

I make all the boys here "*Sons of Liberty.*"* And all the *girls* too! Listen to me, boys and girls! Two days ago, eight hundred Britishers left Boston for Concord to capture our military stores there! —

ALL THE SCHOLARS.

Boo! [*Groans.*]

HALE.

But the Yankees were too smart for them! I want you to give three cheers for Paul Revere, — Ready!

* *A famous club of the day.*

[7]

ALL.

Hip, hip, hip, hooray!

TOM.

[*Excitedly.*] What did he do, sir?

HALE.

He rode like mad to Lexington and warned the people there, and all the farmers on the way, and other men rode in other directions, and when the Britishers came back to Lexington from Concord — [*Stops for breath.*]

ALL THE SCHOOL.

[*Excited, and rising in disorder.*] Yes — yes —

HALE.

[*Continues in crescendo.*] They found Minute Men by every fence, inside each house, behind every rock and tree! and the Americans chased those Regulars clean back to Boston, — at least what was left of them, for the British lost two hundred and seventy-three men, and we only eighty-eight! [*The whole school breaks loose in shouting, — whistles, catcalls, cries, applause, jumping up on their chairs and desks, etc.* Lebanon *tries in vain to quell the tumult; finally* Hale *comes to his rescue and silences the scholars; he turns to* Lebanon *questioningly.*]

LEBANON.

Excuse me, Mr. Hale, there are visitors present; Mrs. Knowlton, the lady who wrote you yesterday.

HALE.

Madam. [*Bows.*]

MRS. KNOWLTON.

[*Who has risen, curtseys.*] Sir! Angelica, rise and curtsey. [*To* Hale.] My daughter, of whom I wrote you, sir. [Hale *bows and* Angelica *curtseys.*] Angelica — what a curtsey! Who'd ever think you'd been taught all the fashionable attainments at a guinea a quarter?

HALE.

I'm afraid you find us rather upside down this morning, madam. But I assure you it's nothing compared to what's going on in

[8]

Boston, where the public schools were closed several days last week.

MRS. KNOWLTON.

So I heard, sir, which was one of my reasons for selecting New London. Sit down, Angelica. [Angelica *sits.*]

HALE.

Excuse me one moment, madam. [*To* Lebanon.] Take Miss —

ANGELICA.

Angelica, sir.

HALE.

Miss Angelica to one side, and inquire about her studies.

LEBANON.

This way, Miss. [*They go beside the window up the stage.*]

HALE.

Miss Alice Adams, please come forward. [Alice *rises and comes to* Hale *in front of desk; she assumes an air of innocence, but with a mischievous and conscious twinkle in her eye when she looks at* Hale.] It will be a great pleasure for you, I am sure, to have your cousin with you.

ALICE.

[*Sweetly and conventionally.*] Yes, Mr. Hale. [*She looks into his face, and deliberately winks mischievously at him, biting back a smile.*]

HALE.

[*Coming nearer her and whispers.*] Can I keep you in at recess? Have you done something I may punish you for?

ALICE.

Yes, sir. *I* drew the picture.

HALE.

[*Delighted.*] Good!

ALICE.

But I 'm afraid you 've spoiled it all by not disapproving.

HALE.

Not a bit of it! As *you* 've done it, I 'll disapprove mightily! [*Smiles*

[9]

lovingly at her, and adds, as he goes back to his desk,] Very well —
that is all, Miss Adams. I will give you an opportunity to talk
with your aunt and cousin during recess.

ALICE.

[*About to go, turns back disappointedly, and speaks to him aside.*]
What — are n't you going to punish me?

HALE.

[*Aside to her.*] Certainly, that is only to blind the others. You
know I'm obliged to change my mind rather suddenly about
this picture. [Alice *goes back to her seat.*] Mr. Lebanon! [Le-
banon *joins Hale and they talk together aside.*]

ANGELICA.

[*Joining her mother.*] Oh, mother, he is really beautiful! He
says I know a great deal. [*She stands by her mother, with one arm
about Mrs.* Knowlton.]

MRS. KNOWLTON.

Humph! He must be a fool. One of your mitts is off, child! Why
is that?

ANGELICA.

[*Drawing her hand away.*] He wanted to kiss my hand.

MRS. KNOWLTON.

Put on your mitt, this minute — and remember this, my dear:
you are not here to learn coquetry, but arithmetic, — the French
language if you like, but not French *manners!*

HALE.

In honor of the day, we will omit the first recitation, and recess
will begin at once. [*A general movement and suppressed murmur
of pleasure from all the scholars.*] One moment, however; on second thoughts, I have decided this picture—ahem—is, after all,
very reprehensible. The perpetrator must suffer. Who is the cul-
prit—she—he—[*Correcting himself quickly*] must be punished.

TOM.

[*Before any one else can speak, rises.*] *I* did it, sir.

[10]

ALICE.

[*Rising.*] No, sir, it was I!

HALE.

Miss Adams, I am *surprised!* And deeply as it pains me, I must keep you in during recess.

TOM.

It's a shame! [*Turns to school.*] He's always doing it!

HALE.

Silence, Master Adams! Ten minutes' recess. [*All the scholars rise, get their hats and caps from pegs on the wall, and go out talking and laughing gaily, except* Tom, *who goes out slowly, angry; and* Alice, *who remains behind.*]

MRS. KNOWLTON.

[*To* Angelica, *as the scholars are leaving.*] I think he is rather strict with your cousin. You'll have to mind your P's and Q's, my dear.

ANGELICA.

I don't like him one-half as much as Mr. Lebanon.

MRS. KNOWLTON.

[*Snapping her fingers on* Angelica's *shoulder.*] Tut, my bird! Enough of that person.

HALE.

[*Rising and turning to Mrs.* Knowlton.] Madam, if you will allow Mr. Lebanon, he will escort you and your daughter about the play-grounds.

MRS. KNOWLTON.

[*Rising.*] Thank you! Can my daughter remain to-day, sir? Angelica, straighten your fichu strings. You do give me the fidgets!

HALE.

Certainly, madam. Mr. Lebanon — [Lebanon *offers his arm to Mrs.* Knowlton, *who takes it after a curtsey to Mr.* Hale.]

MRS. KNOWLTON.

Come, Angelica, and don't drop your mantilla! [Angelica, *after*

[11]

a curtsey, takes Mrs. Knowlton's *hand and they go out — all three.*
Hale *and* Alice *watch them closely till they are off and the door closes
behind them, then both give a sigh of relief, and smile,* Alice *rising
and* Hale *going to her.*]

HALE.
[*Very happy.*] Well? [*Takes her two hands in his.*]

ALICE.
[*Also very happy.*] Well? [Hale *sits on desk before her,* Alice *back
in her seat.*]

HALE.
I'm afraid your brother is becoming unruly. I'll not be able to
keep you in at recess much longer. You see you're not half bad
enough. [*Smiling.*] I ought *not* to punish you, and all the scholars will soon be perceiving that.

ALICE.
I try my best to think of something really bad to do, but my
very wickedest things are always failures, and turn out so namby-
pamby and half-way good, — I'm ashamed.

HALE.
[*Impulsively.*] You darling!

ALICE.
[*Laughing; delighted, but drawing back in mock fear, and holding
her arithmetic open between them.*] Mr. Hale!

HALE.
[*Seriously passionately, taking the book from her unconsciously and
throwing it aside.*] Alice, did a young man ever tell you that he
loved you?

ALICE.
Yes, sir, —[*taking up her geography.*] several have. [*Looking down
into the book.*]

HALE.
What!

ALICE.

[*Looks up at him coyly, then down again into her book.*] And one of them three times.

HALE.

[*Closing the book in her hands and holding it closed so she will look at him.*] I 'll keep you in three recesses in succession—one for each time.

ALICE.

[*Looks straight into his eyes.*] Then I wish he 'd asked me twice as often.

HALE.

Alice !

ALICE.

It was my cousin Fitzroy ! He says he will persist till he wins, and mother says he will.

HALE.

And you — do you like this cousin Fitzroy ?

ALICE.

If I say I like him, will you keep me in another recess ?

HALE.

[*Moodily.*] I 'll keep you in a dozen.

ALICE.

Then I *love* him !

HALE.

[*Forgetting everything but her words, and leaving her.*] Alice — Alice — go, join the others. I 'll never keep you in again.

ALICE.

No — no — you *must !* [*She throws away the geography.*] You promised if I would say I liked my cousin Fitzroy, you 'd keep me in a dozen recesses. [Hale *goes back to her.*] It isn't treating me fair.

HALE.

Do you know what I wish ? I wish life were one long recess and I could keep you in with me forever.

[13]

ALICE.

[*Shyly looking down, speaks softly, naïvely.*] Well — why — don't — you — sir?

HALE.

[*Eagerly, delighted.*] May I?

ALICE.

As if you didn't *know* you could. Only there is one thing —

HALE.

[*Tenderly.*] What is it?

ALICE.

When we're married, I think it 's only fair that *I* should turn the tables, and sometimes *keep you in !*

HALE.

Agreed ! I 'll tell you what —

ALICE.

[*Interrupting.*] Oh ! I have an idea.

HALE.

So have I. . . . I wonder if they're not the same?

ALICE.

I'll try again to do something really naughty !

HALE.

And I will keep you after school.

ALICE.

[*Rises.*] *My* idea — and then you will walk home with me —

HALE.

My idea, too ! And I will ask your father to-day !

ALICE.

[*With a half-mocking curtsey.*] And if he won't give me to you, you will kindly take me all the same, sir.
[*The school-bell rings outside.*]

HALE.

Here come the scholars ! You love me, Alice?

[14]

ALICE.

Yes.

HALE.

Half as much as I love you?

ALICE.

No, *twice* as much!

HALE.

That couldn't be. My love for you is full of all the flowers that ever bloomed! of all the songs the birds have ever sung! of all the kisses the stars have given the sky since night was made. [*He kisses her.*]

The door opens and the scholars enter. Hale *goes quickly to his desk.* Alice *buries her face in a book.* Angelica *and* Lebanon *enter together, after the scholars.*

LEBANON.

Mr. Hale, I think I had best point out to Miss Knowlton what her lessons will be,—and shall she sit next to Miss Adams, sir?

HALE.

Yes. And the first class in grammar will now come forward. [*Seven scholars come forward and take their places on the forms in front of* Hale, *and while they are doing so* Lebanon *has arranged* Angelica *at a desk in front of* Alice.]

LEBANON.

This will be your desk, Miss Angelica.

ANGELICA.

Thank you, sir. Can I see you from here?

LEBANON.

Yes, I always occupy Mr. Hale's chair. But you mustn't look at me *all* the time, young lady.

ANGELICA.

I'll try not to, sir. [*She sighs.* Hale *begins to hear his class.* Lebanon *bends over* Angelica, *opening several books, marking places in them for her, etc. He is showing her where her lessons are to be.*]

[15]

HALE.

Master Tom Adams.

TOM.

[*Rising.*] Yes, sir.

HALE.

The positive, comparative and superlative of good?

TOM.

Good, better, best.

HALE.

Yes. I wish you 'd try and act on one or two of those in school. [Tom *sits, grinning.*] Master Talbot! [Talbot Boy *rises.*] Positive, comparative and superlative of sick?

TALBOT BOY *(who lisps)*.

Thick ——?

HALE.

Well? [*Pause.*] Why, any boy half as old as you could answer that. There 's our little visitor, Master Jefferson there, I 'll wager he knows it. Master Jefferson! [*The* Jefferson Boy *comes forward.*] Positive, comparative and superlative of sick?

THE JEFFERSON BOY.

Sick — [*Pause.*] Worse — [*Longer pause.*] Dead! [*The school laughs.*]

HALE.

[*Laughing.*] That 's a good answer for the son of a doctor to make. [*He nods to the boy to sit, and he does so.*] What is it? [*He looks about and sees* Angelica *and* Lebanon *engrossed in each other behind a grammar book.*] Miss Angelica — [Angelica *and* Lebanon *start.*] Can *you* give it to us?

ANGELICA.

[*Timidly, rising.*] I love — you love — he or she loves. [*The school giggles.*]

HALE.

That was hardly my question, Miss Angelica. [She *sits, embar-*

[16]

rassed. A slight commotion is heard outside.] What I asked was —
[*The door bursts open and* Fitzroy *enters. He is a young handsome fellow of about twenty-five, in the uniform of a British officer ; he is excited, and somewhat loud and noisy.*]

FITZROY.

Is this the Union Grammar School?

HALE.

[*Rising.*] Yes !

FITZROY.

I have been sent here by General Gage, who is in Boston, to hold a meeting of your townspeople who are loyal to King George.

HALE.

What for ?

FITZROY.

Boston is in a state of siege. The rebels who chased the Regulars through Lexington have been joined by other colonists around, and have cut the town completely off from all communication, except by sea. This state of affairs is nothing else than war, and Great Britain calls upon her loyal children !

HALE.

And my schoolhouse ?

FITZROY.

Is where the meeting is to be held, at once.

HALE.

[*Coming down from platform.*] A *Tory* meeting ! Here ! Have you been properly empowered ?

FITZROY.

[*Flourishing a paper.*] Yes, here is my permit. A crier is going about the town now, calling the men to meet within the hour.

HALE.

A Tory meeting here ! [*He turns to the school.*] Then we'll get out, eh, boys ?

[17]

ALL THE SCHOOL.

Yes — yes!

FITZROY.

What — are you all *rebels* here? [*Looking over the school.*]

TOM.

No! We 're "Sons of Liberty!"

FITZROY.

Damn you! [Hale *interrupts him with a gesture, motioning to the girls on their side of the room.* Fitzroy *takes off his bearskin hat and bows gracefully.*] I 'll warrant the young ladies favor the British — What, Alice, — you here? You will allow me, sir? [Hale *bows assent, but not too pleased, and* Fitzroy *goes to* Alice.]

HALE.

What do you say now, Mr. Lebanon? Are *you* going to stay for this meeting?

LEBANON.

No, sir-ee. I am going out to buy a gun.

ANGELICA.

[*Gives an unconscious cry, and forgetting herself and her surroundings, rises frightened, crying,*] Oh, no, Mr. Lebanon, oh, no, no, no!

HALE.

Don't be alarmed, Miss Knowlton! I doubt if he ever uses it.

ANGELICA.

Make him promise me, sir, he 'll never carry it loaded!

HALE.

[*After a jealous look at* Alice *and* Fitzroy, *who are talking together at one side, turns to the school.*] Boys! I have a proposition to make. What do you say to joining a small volunteer company with me at your head? Every boy over fifteen eligible.

BOYS.

Yes — yes!

[18]

THE JEFFERSON BOY.

Please, Mr. Hale, make it boys over 'leven.

HALE.

We 'll make you drummer-boy, Master Jefferson. Come — all boys who want to join, sign this paper. [*They all crowd around the desk and sign, the constant murmur of their voices being heard through the following scene.* Fitzroy *and* Alice *come down stage together,* Alice *leading,* Fitzroy *following.*]

ALICE.

Please do not ask me that again. I tell you, you can *never* persuade me. Nor can my mother influence me the least in this. Twenty mothers couldn't make my heart beat for you, if you can't make it beat yourself. And even if I did love you — [*She adds quickly,*] which I *don't* — I 'd let my heart *break* before I 'd marry a man who is willing to take up arms against his own country !

FITZROY.

That 's a girl's reasoning. England is too great a power to be defeated by an upstart little government like the American, and when she wins, those of us who have stood by her will be rewarded ! These poor rebel fools will have their every penny confiscated, while I have a grant of land, promotion in the army — who knows, perhaps a *title*. Don't refuse me again too quickly !

ALICE.

Too quickly ! There are no words short enough for me to use. You may *sell* your country for money and power, if you like, but you can't buy *me* with it, also. And that 's the last word I 'll ever say to you, Guy Fitzroy.

FITZROY.

Huh ! You 'll change your mind some day ! I mean to *have* you, — do you hear me? If I can't beg or buy you, then I 'll steal. You know what I 'm like when I 'm in my cups ! Some day when I 've made up my mind I can't wait any longer, I 'll drink my-

[19]

self mad for you, and then beware of me. You remember that evening two months ago, after your mother's punch, when I dragged you behind the window curtain and kissed you against your will on your arms and neck and lips till you called for help? Remember that, and don't think you can refuse me carelessly, and have it done with. No, watch for me. [*She stands facing him haughtily, showing her disgust for him. There is a moment's pause in which he gazes passionately and determinedly at her. Fitzroy by a gesture and a toss of his head, as much as to say, "We'll see, I am sure to win," breaks the pause and the feeling of the scene, looking at his watch and speaking as boys go back in single file to their places, having signed the volunteer roll-call.*] It only lacks fifteen minutes of noon; I must be off. I will be back, Mr. Hale, for the meeting at twelve. How many of you boys wish to stay and rally round King George's flag? [*He waits for some sign from the boys. There is only silence.*] You little fools! [*He turns to* Hale.] Is this *your* teaching?

HALE.
Not altogether, though I've done my best, sir. There is a gentleman in the Virginia Assembly who said "Cæsar"—[*He looks at boys with a look and nod of invitation to join him, and they all finish with him heartily.*] "Cæsar had his Brutus, Charles the First his Cromwell, and George III." — [Tom *throws up his cap.*]

FITZROY.
[*Loudly.*] Treason — this is treason!

HALE.
"George III. may profit by their example." That's what Patrick Henry said.

FITZROY.
Fortunate for him he went no farther!

HALE.
Oh, he is still moving! I think he will go far enough before he stops.

FITZROY.

He may go up ! [*With a motion across the throat, of hanging.*] See that the house is ready for us. [Hale *nods*. Fitzroy *looks hard at* Alice, *then says*,] Good day to you all! [*and goes out.*]

HALE.

The school will assemble to-morrow as usual. Of course, if there's really any fighting to be done I shall go, and the boys who are too young to go with me —

THE JEFFERSON BOY.

None of us are, sir.

ALL THE BOYS.

None of us ! none of us !

HALE.

Ah, I 'm *proud* of you ! Proud of you all ! But your parents have something to say; and for the girls and the younger boys we must find another teacher.

LEBANON.

I will stay, Mr. Hale. I feel it 's my duty.

HALE.

[*Amused.*] Ahem ! Very well — that is settled then. For to-day the school is now dismissed, except Miss Alice Adams, who must remain behind.

TOM.

[*Rises, angrily.*] What for? She hasn't done anything — she hasn't had a chance to do anything. You kept her in all recess, and you shan't keep her in again ! [Alice *and* Hale *are secretly amused. The school looks on surprised and excited.*]

HALE.

Look here, Master Adams, what right have you to say as to what shall or shall not be done in this school ?

TOM.

She 's my sister, and you 're always punishing her, and I won't have it !

HALE.

[*Amused.*] Oh, won't you?

TOM.

No, sir, I won't! She never does anything worth being punished
for. You 've got a grudge against her; all the boys have seen it!
Haven't you, boys? Go on, speak out, — haven't you seen it?
[*Turning to the boys, who murmur, rather timidly,*] Yes.

HALE.

Really — May I ask who is master here? School is dismissed,
except Miss Alice Adams, — she remains behind.

TOM.

[*Excited, coming out from his seat to in front of the benches.*] I say
she shan't!

HALE.

And I say it 's none of your business, sir, and she shall.

TOM.

[*Off his head with excitement.*] She shan't! [*Beginning to take off
his coat.*] Will you fight it out with me? Come on — a fair fight!

ALICE.

Tom!
[*The school rise and go out slowly with* Lebanon, *but casting curious looks behind them as they go.* Alice, Hale, *and* Tom *are left behind.*]

HALE.

I will leave it with Miss Adams herself whether she does as I
say, or not.

TOM.

Come on, Alice, come on with me.

ALICE.

No, I prefer to stay.

TOM.

Bah — just like a girl! Very well, then *I* shall stay, too. [Hale
and Alice *look surprised and disappointed, yet secretly amused.*] Every

time you punish my sister, you 'll have to punish me now. If she stays behind, I stay too, to keep her company. [*Behind* Tom's *back* Alice *and* Hale *exchange amused and puzzled looks and affectionate signals. Finally* Hale *has an idea.*]

HALE.

Tom, come here, — go to the blackboard. [Tom *goes sullenly to the board.*] I think we 'll have a little Latin out of you. Write the present tense of the Latin word to love. [Tom *sneers, but with a piece of chalk writes,*

> "Amo, *I love,*
> Amas, *Thou lovest,*
> Amat, *He* —"

is interrupted.] Never mind the "he or she"; just make it "she." [Tom *puts an* "*s*" *in front of the* "*he,*" *making it* "*she,*"*and adds* "*loves.*" Tom *looks sullen and rather foolish, not understanding.* Hale *goes to board and taking a piece of chalk adds after first line* "Alice," *and also to end of second line* "Alice;" *he adds to third line* "me," *and signs it* "Nathan Hale." *The blackboard then reads :* —

> "Amo, *I love* Alice,
> Amas, *Thou lovest* Alice,
> Amat, *She loves* — me.
>   Nathan Hale."]

TOM.

¯*Embarrassed, surprised, not altogether pleased.*] What — I don't believe it — it isn't true !

ALICE.

Rising and coming forward.] Yes, it is, Tom.

TOM.

Well, I 'll be blowed ! — [*He stops short, crimson in the face, and rushes from the room.* Hale *goes toward* Alice *with his arms outstretched to embrace her ;* Alice *goes into his arms — a long embrace and kiss ; a loud tattoo on a drum outside startles them.*]

[23]

HALE.

The Tory meeting!

ALICE.

Fitzroy will be back. I don't want to see him!

HALE.

Quick—we'll go by the window! [*Putting a chair under the window, he jumps onto chair and out; then leans in the window and holds out his hands to Alice, who is on the chair.*] And if to-morrow another drum makes me a soldier—?

ALICE.

It will make me a soldier's sweetheart!

HALE.

Come. [*She gets out of the window with his help, and with loud drum tattoo and bugle call, the Stage is left empty, and the Curtain Falls.*]

Act the Second

Act the Second

SEPTEMBER, 1776. *At Colonel* Knowlton's *house on Harlem Heights. A large, general room with white walls and columns. The furniture of the room is heavy mahogany upholstered in crimson brocade, this latter material also hanging in curtains at the windows. Life-sized portraits by Copley and Stuart, of Colonel and Mrs.* Knowlton *at the time of their marriage, hang on each side of the room. A broad window at back shows the brick wall of the garden, and through a tall, ornamental, iron gate is caught a glimpse of the river. Mrs.* Knowlton *is nervously looking out of the window. She comes from the window, pulls the bell-rope, and returns agitatedly to window. A happy old colored servant in a light blue and silver livery enters in answer.*

SERVANT.

YAAS, m'm?

MRS. KNOWLTON.
Oh, Jasper, how long since Miss Angelica went out?

SERVANT.
I dunno, m'm.

MRS. KNOWLTON.
It isn't safe for her to go out alone, Jasper.

SERVANT.
No, m'm.

MRS. KNOWLTON.
[*Looking again out of window.*] And I've expressly forbidden her.

SERVANT.
Yaas, m'm.

MRS. KNOWLTON.
[*Turning and coming back excitedly on her toes.*] And you don't know?

SERVANT.

Dunno nothing, m'm.

MRS. KNOWLTON.

And the other servants?

SERVANT.

None of the servants in this hyah house, m'm, dunno nothing whatsomever what ole Jasper dunno.

[*Colonel* Knowlton *enters hurriedly. He is a tall, striking-looking man, aquiline features, and iron-gray hair. He is strong in character, brave in spirit, and affectionate in heart. He is dressed in the blue and buff uniform of a Revolutionary Colonel.*]

COLONEL KNOWLTON.

[*Speaks as he enters.*] Ah, Martha, that's good I've found you!

SERVANT.

[*Eagerly.*] Beg pardon, sah, but am thar any news, Colonel?

COLONEL KNOWLTON.

Yes, Jasper. You servants must turn all our rooms into bed-chambers by to-night. [*Sits heavily on the sofa as if he were tired.*]

MRS. KNOWLTON.

What! [*Going to him and sitting beside him on the sofa.*]
[*Jasper leaves the room, taking the Colonel's sword and hat.*]

COLONEL KNOWLTON.

The army has abandoned the city, under Washington's orders, to take a position here, on Harlem Heights. Washington is making his own headquarters at the house of Robert Murray, on Murray Hill, and we must take in all the staff officers we can.

MRS. KNOWLTON.

[*Brushing the dust off his shoulders, and holding his arm affectionately.*] Well, I'm glad of a chance to be of some sort of use, even if it's only to turn the house into a tavern! Have we abandoned the city entirely?

COLONEL KNOWLTON.

No, General Putnam is there with four thousand men. But every-

Act Second

one who can is leaving. The sick have been sent over to Paulus Hook.* I told Captain Adams he should stay with us, and he brings Alice with him.

MRS. KNOWLTON.

That's most desirable for Angelica. This Lebanon person proposed for her again to me this morning! He doesn't seem to understand the meaning of the word "No." The next time *you'd* better say it and see if he *will* understand.

COLONEL KNOWLTON.

What is there against Mr. Lebanon?—Where is Angelica?

MRS. KNOWLTON.

I don't know, and I'm that worried. [*Rises and goes again to the window.*] She's been gone two hours, and she didn't wear her pattens.

JASPER.

[*Enters, announcing,*] Captain Adams, sah, and Missy. [*Colonel Knowlton rises as Captain Adams and Alice come in. Alice looks much more of a young lady than in the first act, and very charming in a full blue and white dress, big hat, and black silk pelisse for travelling. Her father, Captain Adams, is a portly, dignified, good-hearted man, older than Colonel Knowlton, and like him in colonial uniform. Captain Adams kisses Mrs. Knowlton, then goes to Knowlton, while Alice kisses Mrs. Knowlton.*]

MRS KNOWLTON.

I'm so glad you came, too, Alice. Angelica is worrying me terribly. [*Helping Alice off with her pelisse. The two women go up the stage together.*]

CAPTAIN ADAMS.

I've been seeing about the public stores which are being taken to Dobb's Ferry. General Washington tells me he has asked you to hold a conference here to-day.

* *Now Jersey City.*

COLONEL KNOWLTON.
Yes. [*Turning to Mrs.* Knowlton.] We must prepare this room, Martha.

MRS. KNOWLTON.
What is the conference for?

COLONEL KNOWLTON.
We must discover, in some way, what the enemy's plans are.

CAPTAIN ADAMS.
Yes, what are these damned British going to do? We *must* know. The army is becoming more and more demoralized every day.

ALICE.
Only to think! We 've heard our soldiers are actually in need of the barest necessities of clothing, and there are practically no blankets. [*During* Alice's *speech, Mrs.* Knowlton *goes to the door at left, opens it and listens for* Angelica. *Closes it and comes back.*]

MRS. KNOWLTON.
No blankets—and the winter coming! Well! I was married with six pairs, and mother was married with six, and Angelica shan't be married at all—at least not till this war 's over! So there 's three times six,—eighteen pairs for the Continental soldiers—bless their hearts! Alice, how about young Fitzroy? It 's rumored again you 're going to marry him. [*Crossing to* Alice *as she speaks her name. At the same time the two men go a few steps up the stage and talk together confidentially.*]

ALICE.
Oh, that rumor spreads every time I refuse him; and I did again by post, yesterday.

MRS. KNOWLTON.
I 'm glad of it! He 's nothing like Captain Hale's equal. People aren't through talking yet of *his* gallant capture of the British sloop in the East River!

COLONEL KNOWLTON.
Hale 's done a hundred brave things since then! The eyes of the whole army are upon him.

Act Second

ALICE.

[*Very happy and proud.*] I know something very few are aware of. Not long ago the men of his company, whose term of service had expired, determined to leave the ranks, and he offered to give them his pay if they would only remain a certain time longer. [*The two men come forward.*]

CAPTAIN ADAMS.

Good heavens! What, my daughter doesn't know about Captain Hale!—

ALICE.

[*Beseeching.*] Father!

CAPTAIN ADAMS.

[*Smiling.*] If you allow Alice, she will spend the day discanting on Captain Hale's merits. As for Fitzroy, he's a blackguard. They say he would like to join the Americans now, but don't dare, because he killed one of his old friends in a drunken brawl, and he's afraid he'd get strung for it.

COLONEL KNOWLTON.

And just at present, Martha, Captain Adams would probably be pleased to go to his room.

MRS. KNOWLTON.

By all means. This way, Captain. Alice, I will return for you in a moment. You must share with Angelica, now the house is to be turned into a barracks.

COLONEL KNOWLTON.

Be careful you girls don't do any wounding on your own account. We've no men to spare. [Alice *laughs.* Mrs. Knowlton *and Captain* Adams *go out by the door, left.* Alice *stops Colonel* Knowlton, *as he is about to follow. She pantomimes him to come back, pushes him down onto the sofa—she is behind it—and with her arms about his neck, speaks cajolingly.*]

ALICE.

Uncle Knowlton?

[31]

COLONEL KNOWLTON.

Yes, my dear.

ALICE.

Have you any news of Captain Hale?

COLONEL KNOWLTON.

How long is it since you have seen him?

ALICE.

Much too long, and I 've made up my mind not to have it any more.

COLONEL KNOWLTON.

That 's right, don't trust him. In Connecticut, where he 's been, the girls are far too pretty. [*Insinuatingly, bending his head back and looking up at her humorously.*]

ALICE.

[*Jealously.*] You 've heard some stories of him?

COLONEL KNOWLTON.

[*Teasing her.*] Ahem! Far be it from me to expose a fellow soldier.

ALICE.

Uncle Knowlton, I 'm ashamed of you! An old man like you!

COLONEL KNOWLTON.

Oh, not so old!

ALICE.

What do you know?

COLONEL KNOWLTON.

[*Rising.*] Nothing, my dear. I was only jesting. [*Starting to go.*]

ALICE.

I 'm not so sure of that. Wait a minute! [*Coming from behind the sofa to him, she seizes hold of him by a button on the breast of his coat, taking a pair of scissors from the table—the house bell is heard.*]

COLONEL KNOWLTON.

What are you doing?

[32]

ALICE.

Getting a soldier's button to make Captain Hale jealous with !
He shan't think he is the only one to flirt.
[Jasper *enters from the hall in answer to the house bell and crosses
the room to the door which leads to upstairs.*]

COLONEL KNOWLTON.

We soldiers don't *give* buttons away—we sell them !

ALICE.

Oh, I 'm going to kiss you ! You 're quite old enough for that,
[*She kisses him.*] but, when I tell Nathan about it, I shall pretend
you were somebody else, and young, and good looking !
[Jasper, *who has watched them by the doorway, right, chuckles and
goes out.*]

COLONEL KNOWLTON.

Well, you can tell him to-day if you like !—[*For a second* Alice
*cannot speak for surprise and joy ; then she catches her breath and
cries,*]

ALICE.

He 's coming here !

COLONEL KNOWLTON.

Yes. [*Nods his head violently.*]

ALICE.

Oh ! [*She cries out for very happiness, and running across the room
throws herself in an ecstasy of joy upon the sofa ; then quickly jumps
up and runs back to Colonel* Knowlton.] I 'll kiss you again for
that good news. [*Starts to kiss him ; changes her mind.*] No, I won't,
either !

COLONEL KNOWLTON.

No, you must save all the rest of your kisses for Captain Hale !

ALICE.

Oh, dear no ! Yours weren't at all the kind I give him. You know
there are two kinds of visits,—those we make because we want
to see people, and those we make on strangers, or after a party,

whether we want to or not. The latter are called *duty visits!*
'Well?—Do you understand?

COLONEL KNOWLTON.

No, not in the least.

ALICE.

Stupid! Your *kiss* was a *duty visit.* [*With a low mocking curtsey.*]
What hour is he coming?

COLONEL KNOWLTON.

I won't tell you, Miss! I won't give you another party, all for that
one little duty visit. [*And he starts to go out by the door, left.*]

MRS. KNOWLTON.

[*Off the stage, left, calls,*] Thomas!

COLONEL KNOWLTON.

Coming, Martha! [*He closes the door behind him.*]

ALICE.

[*Dances half-way around the room, singing,*]
        " Nathan is coming, to-day, to-day!
        Nathan is coming to-day, to-day!" etc., etc.
[*Till she reaches the mirror on the wall at the left. She examines herself critically in the glass, still singing, takes a rose from a vase and
puts it in her hair, retouches her toilet where she can, and pinches
her cheeks to make them red.*] Oh, dear, I wish I were prettier! I
wonder what those Connecticut girls are like!—[*Angelica
appears outside the window, and thrusts her head in.*]

ANGELICA.

[*Whispers.*] Alice!

ALICE.

[*Startled.*] Oh! Angelica!

ANGELICA.

Sh!.... don't look—turn your head the other way.

ALICE.

What in the world—!

ANGELICA.

Sh—Go on—Please.... [*Alice turns her back to the window.*

[34]

Act Second

Angelica *beckons, off left, and runs past the window, followed by* Lebanon, *quickly. The front door is heard to slam.* Angelica *puts her head in at the doorway, right.*]

ALICE.

What's the matter?

ANGELICA.

Alice! Matter! Matter enough! I'm married!!

ALICE.

[*Loudly.*] What!!

ANGELICA.

[*Frightened.*] Sh! Where is mother?

ALICE.

Upstairs.

ANGELICA.

Very well. [*Speaks over her shoulder.*] Come along, darling! [*She enters, followed by* Lebanon, *dressed in Continental uniform. He wears a white wedding favor, and carries a gun awkwardly.*] I'm a married woman, Alice! [*She turns and directs* Alice's *attention to* Lebanon, *on whom she gazes lovingly.*] Isn't he beautiful in his soldier clothes? [Lebanon *smiles, embarrassed but happy, and goes to shake hands with* Alice.] Go on, you can kiss him, Alice. I won't be jealous, just this once on our wedding day!

LEBANON.

[*To* Angelica.] No, really, thank you, Precious, but I'd rather not. [*To* Alice.] You don't mind?

ALICE.

[*Smiling.*] Oh, no, pray don't put yourself out for me!

ANGELICA.

[*Aside to* Lebanon.] You've hurt her feelings. [*She tries to take his arm, but it is his right in which he carries his gun. Aloud.*] Hold your gun in your other hand, I want to take your arm. [*He changes his gun awkwardly. They stand together, arm in arm, her head on his shoulder, and she gives a happy sigh.*] Alice, will you break it to mother, at once?

[35]

ALICE.

Mercy! I forgot about that. It's an elopement!

ANGELICA.

Yes, and in the day time! I hated to do without a moon, but I could never get away evenings.

ALICE.

Does your mother suspect?

ANGELICA.

Not a sign. She refused Ebenezer again this morning!

MRS. KNOWLTON.

[*Calls from off stage, left.*] Alice! [*All start.* Angelica *and* Lebanon *show* abjeſt *terror, and,* "*grabbing*" *for each other, cling together.*]

ANGELICA.

Oh, she's coming! Save us. Alice, save us!

ALICE.

Quick! Go back into the hall. [*Starts pushing them out.*]

LEBANON.

Do it gently, Miss Alice.

ANGELICA.

Yes, mother couldn't stand too great a shock. [*They go out, right.* Alice *takes a ribbon out of the little bag she carries, and putting* Colonel Knowlton's *button on it, ties it around her neck, as Mrs.* Knowlton *comes into the room.*]

MRS. KNOWLTON.

I heard voices. What did they want?

ALICE.

[*Embarrassed, but amused.*] They desired me to tell you, as gently as possible, that they—that she—that he—well, that *you* are a *mother-in-law!*

MRS. KNOWLTON.

What do you mean, child, by calling me names?

[36]

Act Second

ALICE.

Angelica—

MRS. KNOWLTON.

Angelica!—Mother-in-law—Alice, don't tell me! Give me air!
Give me air!

ALICE.

[*Fanning her.*] Air!

MRS. KNOWLTON.

No! no! I mean something to sit on. Angelica—my baby!
hasn't made herself miserable for life? [*Sitting in a chair which
Alice brings forward for her.*]

ALICE.

No! She 's married.

MRS. KNOWLTON.

It 's the same thing! Who was the wicked child's accomplice?
[*She suddenly realizes, and rises.*] It wasn't—it wasn't—that—
[*She chokes.*] that—*that!* —

ALICE.

Lebanon!

MRS. KNOWLTON.

No! [*Her legs give way, owing to her emotions, and she sits suddenly in the chair.*] I won't believe it! Those children! I 'll spank
them both and put them to bed! No! I won't do that either!
Where are they?

ALICE.

In the hall.

MRS. KNOWLTON.

[*Rises and gestures tragically.*] Call them!

ALICE.

[*Going to the door, right.*] You won't be cruel to her—[*Mrs.*
Knowlton *breathes hard through her tightly compressed lips.*]
Angelica! [Angelica *and* Lebanon *enter timidly.*]

ANGELICA.

Mother!

[37]

MRS. KNOWLTON.

Don't come near me! I—you undutiful child! [*She begins to break down and tears threaten her;— to* Lebanon,] As for you, sir—words fail me—I [*She breaks down completely, and turns to* Angelica.] Oh, come to my arms! [*The last is meant for* Angelica *only, but* Lebanon *takes it for himself also. Both* Angelica *and* Lebanon *go to Mrs.* Knowlton's *arms, but she repulses* Lebanon.] Not you, sir! Not *you!* [*And enfolds* Angelica.] My little girl! Why did you?—[*Crying.*]

ANGELICA.

[*Herself a little tearful.*] He said he'd go fight if I'd marry him! And I heard so much of our needing soldiers; I did it, a little, for the sake of the country!

MRS. KNOWLTON.

Rubbish! Come to my room!—

ANGELICA.

Look at him, mother! And I wouldn't marry him till he put them all on! Gun and all!

LEBANON.

[*Timidly.*] Mother!

MRS. KNOWLTON.

[*Turning.*] *What!!* How dare you, sir!

LEBANON.

Please be a mother to me, just for a few minutes. I'm going off to fight this evening.

MRS. KNOWLTON.

[*Witheringly.*] Fight! You?

LEBANON.

Yes, I said to my wife—[*These words very proudly.* Angelica *also straightens up at them, and Mrs.* Knowlton *gasps angrily.*] Let's begin with your mother, and if I'm not afraid before her, I'll be that much encouraged toward facing the British. [Angelica, *seizing* Lebanon's *free hand, says* "Come," *and the two kneel at Mrs.* Knowlton's *feet, in the manner of old-fashioned story books.*]

Forgive him, mother, for the sake of the country

ANGELICA.

Forgive him, mother, for the sake of the country?

MRS. KNOWLTON.

Hm! We'll see—[*She goes out saying,*] Come, Angelica! [Angelica *follows her out, beckoning to* Lebanon *to follow, which he does, pushed forward by* Alice. Alice *is left alone.* Jasper *enters from the right.*]

JASPER.

Has Colonel Knowlton gone out, Missy?

ALICE.

No, Jasper.

JASPER.

'Cause thah's a young Captain Hale hyah to pay his respecks.

ALICE.

Captain Hale!

JASPER.

Yaas, Missy.

ALICE.

Then never you mind about Colonel Knowlton, Jasper; *I* will take all the respects that gentleman has to pay!

JASPER.

La, Missy! Is you sweet on him? [*Opens door.*] This way, sah! Hyah's a young lady says as how she's been waiting up sence sunrise foa you!

ALICE.

Jasper! [*Hale enters.*]

HALE.

[*Seeing her, is very much surprised.*] Alice! [*He rushes to her and takes her in his arms.*]

JASPER.

[*By the door, right, with much feeling.*] Dat's right, kiss on, ma honeys! Smack each other straight from the heart. It does ole Jasper good to see you. Thah's a little yaller gal lying out in the graveyard, yonder, dat knows ole Jasper was fond of kissing, too! [Alice *and* Hale *finish their embrace, and sit side by*

[39]

Nathan Hale

side on the sofa. They are unconscious of Jasper's *presence, who lingers to enjoy their love, unable to tear himself away. He speaks softly to himself.*] Don't stop, ma honeys, don't stop !

HALE.

I had no hint I should find you here. [*Taking her hand.*]

ALICE.

Father brought me to-day.

JASPER.

[*Taking a step nearer to them behind the sofa.*] Bress their little souls !

HALE.

I have just come down from Connecticut—a lovely part of the country. [Alice *draws her hand away.*]

ALICE.

Yes. I 've heard of you there.

JASPER.

[*Coming in earshot, disappointed.*] Oh, go on, ma honeys, don't stop ! Kiss again, jes' for ole Jasper's sake !

ALICE.

Jasper !

HALE.

What do you want, Jasper ?

JASPER.

Want to see you kiss again, Cappen. It warms ma ole heart, it does.

HALE.

[*Laughing.*] I 'll warm something else for you, if you don't get out !

JASPER.

You don' mind ole Jasper, Cappen ? Why, I done see the nobles' in the lan' kiss right yah in this very room !

HALE.

Well, you go away now. You have kissing on the brain.

[40]

Act Second

JASPER.

Maybe I has, Cappen, but I 'd a deal sight rather have it on the lips! You ain't the on'y sojer anyway, Cappen, what Missy 's kissed. Take ole Jasper's word for dat, you ain't the on'y one this very day, you take ole Jasper's word for dat! [*Chuckling.*]

ALICE.

[*Leading* Jasper *on to make* Hale *jealous.*] Why, Jasper, where were you?

JASPER.

I was jes' comin' in, Missy, and jes' goin' out. I shet my eyes tight, but they would squint, honey! Jasper's ears anyway are jes' as sartin as stealin' to hear kissin' goin' on anywhere round these hyah parts. [*He goes out, right.*]

HALE.

Is that true? [Alice *looks at him, smiling provokingly, and playing with the military button on the ribbon around her neck, to call his attention to it. He sees the button.*] Whose—[*He stops himself, resolved not to ask her about it; but he can't take his eyes off it.*]

ALICE.

I wish to ask a question or two! How many young ladies did you see in Connecticut?

HALE.

[*Moodily.*] I don't know. What soldier's button is that you wear on your neck?

ALICE.

What young ladies have you made love to, since we 've been separated?

HALE.

Whom did you kiss to-day, before me?

ALICE.

Confess!

HALE.

Whom?

[41]

ALICE.

[*Rises.*] Captain Hale, [*With a curtsey.*] I 'm not your pupil any longer, to be catechised so !

HALE.

[*Rises also.*] Very well ! Please tell your uncle, Colonel Knowlton, I am here to see him.

ALICE.

Captain Hale, [*Another curtsey.*] I shan't do any such thing.

HALE.

Then I 'll go find him myself. [*Going toward the door, left.*]

ALICE.

[*Running before him.*] No, you won't—Captain Hale—[*Going before the door and barring his way.*]

HALE.

Give me that button. [*His eyes on it.*]

ALICE.

[*Leaning against the door-frame.*] Not for worlds ! [*Kissing it.*]

HALE.

[*Looking about the room.*] I 'll climb out the window. [Alice *runs to prevent him, and gets to the window first.*]

ALICE.

Do, if you like, but I shan't follow you *this time !*

HALE.

Ah, you remember that day in the schoolhouse when you promised to be a soldier's sweetheart ? I didn't know you meant a whole regiment's.

ALICE.

[*Coming away from the window, indignant.*] How dare you ! Leave my house !

HALE.

Whose house ?

ALICE.

I mean—my uncle's house.

[42]

Act Second

HALE.

Which way may I go? The way I came?

ALICE.

[*Witheringly.*] Yes, back to your Connecticut young ladies!

HALE.

Thank you! [*Bows, and steps out of the low window.* Alice *stands listening a moment, then hurries to the window and leans out, calling.*]

ALICE.

Nathan! Nathan! Where are you going?

HALE.

Where you sent me—to—ahem!—Connecticut!

ALICE.

Are there so many pretty girls there?

HALE.

There isn't a petticoat in the State—at least there wasn't for my eyes!

ALICE.

Then come back! Come back! Quickly! [Nathan *reappears outside the window.*]

HALE.

Aren't you ashamed of yourself?

ALICE.

No!

HALE.

[*Laughingly.*] Then I won't come back!

ALICE.

Very well, sir, don't!

HALE.

What reward will you give me, if I do?

ALICE.

[*Thinks a second.*] This *button!*

HALE.

Good! [*Putting his hands on window ledge, springs in. He holds out his hand for the button.*] Give it to me!

[43]

Nathan Hale

ALICE.

[*Teasing, pretends to be sad and repentant.*] First I must make a confession.

HALE.

[*Depressed.*] Go on.

ALICE.

And tell you *whom* I kissed.

HALE.

[*More depressed.*] Well?

ALICE.

You 'll forgive me?

HALE.
[*Desperate, between his teeth.*] Yes!

ALICE.

[*Looks up, smiling mischievously.*] It was *Uncle Knowlton!* [Hale starts, looks at her a moment, comprehends, then laughs.]

HALE.

You little devil, you! To tease your true love out of his wits. But I will make you regret it — I have been very ill in Connecticut.

ALICE.

That's why you were there so long! [*All her teasing humor vanishes, and for the rest of the act Alice is serious. From this moment in the play the woman in her slowly and finally usurps the girl.*]

HALE.

Yes. As soon as I was able I came on here. I 've been out of the fighting long enough.

ALICE.

Fighting! Is there to be another battle at once? Is that what this conference is for?

HALE.

I don't know, but we must attack or we 'll be driven entirely out of New York, as we were out of Boston.

[44]

Act Second

ALICE.

General Washington has twenty thousand men!

HALE.

Yes, with no arms for half of them, and two-thirds undrilled.
Good Heavens, the patient courage of that man! Each defeat,
he says, only trains his men the better, and fits them for win-
ning victory in the end! But General Howe has crossed now to
Long Island with thirty thousand British soldiers.

ALICE.

Oh, this dreadful war! When will it end?

HALE.

Not till we 've won our freedom, or every man among us is dead
or jailed!

ALICE.

That 's the horror that comes to me at night, Nathan. I see you
starving, choking, in some black hole, with one of those brutes
of a red coat over you, or worse,—lying on the battlefield,
wounded, dying, and *away from me!* There 's one horrible dream
that comes to me often! It came again last week! I 'm in an
orchard, and the trees are pink and white with blossoms, and
the birds are singing, and the air is sweet with spring; then
great clouds of smoke drift through, and the little birds drop
dead from their branches, and the pink petals fall blood-red on
the white face of a soldier lying on the ground, and it 's you—
[*In a hysterical frenzy.*] you!! And—then I wake up, and
oh, my God! I 'm afraid some day it will happen! Nathan!
Nathan!

HALE.

My darling, my darling! It 's only a war dream, such as comes
to every one in times like these! [*Taking her in his arms and
comforting her.*]

ALICE.

Yes, and how often they prove true! Oh, Nathan, must you go
on fighting?

[45]

HALE.

Alice!

ALICE.

Yes, yes, of course you must. I know we need every man we have and more! Ah, if only I were one, to fight by your side, or even a drummer-boy to lead you on! [*She adds with a slight smile, and a momentary return to her girlish humor, and quickly, in a confidential tone, as if she were telling a secret,*] I would be very *careful* where *I led you!* Not where the danger was greatest, I 'll warrant! [*She returns to her former serious mood.*] Nathan, listen. Promise me one thing,—that when you do go back to the fighting, you won't expose yourself unnecessarily.

HALE.

[*Smiling.*] My dear little woman, I don't know what you mean!

ALICE.

Yes, you do! You must! It *isn't* a foolish thing I 'm asking! And I ask it for your love of me! You must fight, of course, and I want you to fight bravely—you couldn't do otherwise, that you 've proved time and again! Well, let it be so! Fight bravely! But promise me you won't let yourself be carried away into leading some forlorn hope, that you won't risk your precious life just to encourage others! Remember, it 's my life now! Don't volunteer to do more than your duty as a soldier demands,— not more, for my sake. Don't willingly place the life I claim for mine in any jeopardy your honor as a soldier does not make imperative. Will you promise me that?

HALE.

Yes, dear, I will promise you that.

ALICE.

That you won't risk your life unnecessarily! Swear it to me!

HALE.

[*Smiling.*] By what?

ALICE.

[*Very serious.*] By your love for me, and mine for you.

HALE.

[*Serious.*] I swear it!

ALICE.

Ah, God bless you! [*In the greatest relief, and with joy, she goes to embrace him, but they stand apart, startled by a loud knocking of the iron knocker on the front door of the house.*]

HALE.

The men, beginning to come for the conference!

ALICE.

Oh, I wish I could stay! Can't I stay?

HALE.

No. No women can be present.

ALICE.

If I asked Uncle?

HALE.

He hasn't the power!
[*Colonel* Knowlton *and Captain* Adams *come into the room from upstairs.*]

COLONEL KNOWLTON.

Ah, Hale, you 're in good time! [*Shakes his hand, and* Hale *passes on and shakes Captain* Adams's *hand, as* Jasper *ushers in three other men in uniform, who are greeted cordially by Colonel* Knowlton, *and who pass on in turn to Captain* Adams *and* Hale, *with whom each also shakes hands. Meanwhile,* Alice, *seeing she is unobserved, steals to the big window recess, where she conceals herself behind the curtains. While the men are greeting each other with the ordinary phrases,* Jasper *speaks at the door, right.*]

JASPER.

[*Shaking his head.*] What a pity Colonel Knowlton was down already! Ole Jasper was jes' a countin' on gittin' another kiss! [*Starts to go out, but stops to hold door open, saying,*] This way, gem-men, if you please. [Hull, *a handsome young officer,* Hale's *age, and another man in uniform enter. They greet, first Colonel* Knowlton *and then the others.*]

COLONEL KNOWLTON.

Jasper, arrange the chairs and table for us.

JASPER.

Yaas, sir. [*He goes about the room arranging chairs and talking aloud to himself. Places table for Colonel Knowlton at right, with a chair behind it, and groups the other chairs in a semicircle on the left. Three more men come in together and two separately, each one shaking hands all around, and always with Colonel Knowlton first.*] Lor' save us, ef I knows how to arrange chahs for dis hyah meetin'! It ain't exackly a gospel meetin', no yetwise a funeral. Mo' like a funeral 'n anything else, I reckon! Funeral o' dat tha British Lion. [*Moving the table.*] Dat's the place for the corpse. [*Placing a chair behind.*] Dat's fo' the preacher, and these hyah other chahs—[*With a final arrangement of the chairs.*] is fo' de mourners! Guess dey's mighty glad to get red o' sech a pesky ole relation, seems as ef she want de mother country, but mo' like de mother-in-law country, to ole Jasper's mind. [*At this moment Colonel Knowlton, looking up, sees that all is ready.*]

COLONEL KNOWLTON.

[*With a motion to the men, and to the chairs.*] Brother soldiers! [*They take their places in the chairs according to their military rank, Hale in the last row behind all the others. Colonel Knowlton takes his chair behind the table. Jasper draws the heavy brocade curtains in front of the window recess, and in so doing discovers Alice. He starts, but, with her finger on her lips, she motions him to be silent. None of the others know she is there. Tom Adams enters in Continental soldier's uniform. He gives the military salute.*]

TOM.

Uncle, may I be present?

COLONEL KNOWLTON.

Yes, my boy, if no one has any objection. [*He looks at the other men, but they all murmur, "Oh, no, no," and "Certainly not," and Tom takes his place beside Hale at the back.*] That is all, Jasper, and we are not to be interrupted.

Act Second

JASPER.

Yaas, sir.

COLONEL KNOWLTON.

Not on pain of imprisonment, Jasper.

JASPER.

Nobody 's not gwine to get into this hyah room, Colonel, with ole Jasper outside the door, not even King George hisself, honey. [*With a stolen look toward the window where* Alice *is hiding, he goes out, right. A moment's important silence. The men are all composed, serious.*]

COLONEL KNOWLTON.

[*Who has taken a letter from his pocket.*] Gentlemen, I will first read you portions of a letter from General Washington to General Heath, forwarded to me with the request from headquarters that I should summon you here to-day. [*He reads.*]"The fate of the whole war depends upon obtaining intelligence of the enemy's motions; I do most earnestly entreat you and General Clinton to exert yourselves to accomplish this most desirable end. I was never more uneasy than on account of my want of knowledge on this score. *It is vital.*" [*He closes the letter, and places it in his breast pocket.*] Gentlemen, General Heath, General Clinton, and General Washington together have decided there is but one thing to be done. [*A moment's pause.*] A competent person must be sent, in *disguise*, into the British camp on Long Island to find out these secrets on which depends *everything!* It must be a man with some experience in military affairs, with some scientific knowledge, a man of education, one with a quick eye, a cool head, and courage,—*unflinching courage!* He will need tact and caution, and, above all, he must be one in whose judgment and fidelity the American Nation may have implicit confidence ! I have summoned those men associated with me in the command of our army whom I personally think capable of meeting all these requirements. To the man who offers his services, in compensation for the risks he must run, is given the opportunity of serving his country supremely! Does any one of the men of this

[49]

company now before me volunteer ? [*He ends solemnly and most impressively. There is a long pause, the men do not move, and keep their faces set, staring before them. After waiting in vain for some one to speak,* Knowlton *continues.*] *Not one?* Have I pleaded so feebly in behalf of my country then? Or have I failed in placing her dire necessity before you? Surely you don't need me to tell you how our Continental Army is weak, wasted, unfed, un-clothed, unsupplied with ammunition. We could not stand a long siege, nor can we stand a sudden combined attack. We must know beforehand and escape from both, should either be planned ! After fighting bravely, as we have, are we to lose all we have gained, the *liberty* within our grasp, at this late day ? No! One of you *will* come forward! What is it your country asks of you? Only to be a hero !

HULL.

No! To be a spy ! [*A murmur of assent from the men.*]

CAPTAIN ADAMS.

There's not a man amongst us who wouldn't lead a handful of men against a regiment of the English! who wouldn't fight for liberty in the very mouth of the cannon! but this is a request not meant for men like us.

HULL.

[*Looking at the other men.*]We are all true patriots here, I take it!

ALL.

Aye ! Aye ! Patriots !

HULL.

[*Appealing to the men.*] Are we the men to be called on to play a part which every nation looks upon with scorn and contumely?

ALL.

No ! No !

HULL.

[*Turning again to* Knowlton.] I would give my *life* for my coun-try, but not my *honor !*

ALL.

Hear ! Hear !

[50]

COLONEL KNOWLTON.

But, do you understand? Do you realize all that's at stake?

ALL.

Yes! Yes!

COLONEL KNOWLTON.

Then surely one of you *will* come forward in response to this desperate appeal from your chief. In the name of Washington, I ask for a volunteer! [*He waits. Silence again. He rises.*] Men! Listen to me! Shall our fathers and brothers killed on the field of battle be sacrificed for nothing? Will you stand still beside their dead bodies and see our hero, George Washington, shot down before your eyes as a traitor? Will you accept oppression again and give up Liberty now you 've won it? Or is there, in the name of God, one man among you to come forward with his *life and his honor* in his hands to lay down, if needs be, for his country? [*After a short pause,* Hale *rises, pale, but calm.*]

HALE.

I will undertake it! [*General surprise not unmixed with consternation, and all murmur, questioningly,* "Hale!" *A short pause.*]

COLONEL KNOWLTON.

Captain Nathan Hale—[Hale *comes forward.*]

CAPTAIN ADAMS.

[*Interrupting, rises.*] I protest against allowing Captain Hale to go on this errand!

HULL.

And I!

ALL.

And I! And I!

CAPTAIN ADAMS.

Captain Hale is too valuable a member of the army for us to risk losing. [*He turns to* Hale.] Hale, you can't do this! You haven't the right to sacrifice the brilliant prospects of your life! The hopes of your family, of your friends, of us, your fellow-soldiers! Let some one else volunteer; you must withdraw your offer. [*A second's pause. All look at* Hale *questioningly.*]

[51]

HALE.

[*Quietly.*] Colonel Knowlton, I repeat my offer!

CAPTAIN ADAMS.

[*Rising, excitedly.*] No! We are all opposed to it! Surely we have some influence with you! It is to certain death that you are needlessly exposing yourself!

HALE.

Needlessly?

HULL.

[*Also rising, excitedly.*] It is to more than certain death, it is to an ignominious one! Captain Hale, as a member of your own regiment, I ask you not to undertake this! [*Hale shakes his head simply.*] We will find some one else! Some one who can be more easily spared. [*Here he loses his manner of soldier, and speaks impulsively as a boy.*] Nathan—dear old man!—We were schoolboys together, and for the love we bore each other then, and have ever since, for the love of all those who love you and whom you hold dear, I beg you to listen to me!

HALE.

[*Looks at* Hull *with a smile of affection and gratitude, and turns to* Knowlton.] I understand, sir, there is no one else ready to perform this business?

COLONEL KNOWLTON.

I must confess there is no one, Captain.

HALE.

Then I say again, I will go.

TOM.

[*Hurrying forward.*] Mr. Hale!—Sir!—Captain! [*Seizes* Hale's *hand.*] For the sake of my sis—[*He is interrupted quickly and suddenly by* Hale, *who places his hand on his mouth to prevent his speaking the rest.* Hale *takes a long breath, sets his face, then gives* Tom's *hand a mighty grip, and puts him behind him.*]

HALE.

[*Who is much moved, but gradually controls himself.*] Gentlemen,

[52]

Act Second

I thank you all for the affection you have shown me, but I think
I owe to my country the accomplishment of an object so important and so much desired by the commander of her armies.
I am fully sensible of the consequences of discovery and capture
in such a situation, but I hold that every kind of service necessary for the public good becomes *honorable* by being *necessary!*
And my country's claims upon me are imperious!
[*Unnoticed by the men,* Alice *draws aside the curtains and comes
slowly forward during Colonel* Knowlton's *following speech.*]

COLONEL KNOWLTON.
[*Rises, and going to* Hale, *shakes his hand with deep feeling.*] Manly,
wise, and patriotic words, sir, which I am sure your country will
not forget! I—I will call for you this afternoon to appear before Washington. Gentlemen, this conference is finished. [*A
general movement of the men is immediately arrested by* Alice's
voice.*]

ALICE.
No! It is not!

CAPTAIN ADAMS.
Alice! [Alice *is white, haggard, "beside herself." She is oblivious
of all but* Hale. *She goes to him, and, seizing his wrist, holds it in
a tight but trembling grasp.*]

ALICE.
[*In a low, hoarse whisper.*] Your promise to me! Your promise!

HALE.
[*Surprised.*] Do you hold me to it?

ALICE.
Yes!

HALE.
Then I must break it!

ALICE.
No! I refuse to free you. You have given two years of your
life to your country. It must give me the rest. It's my share!
It's my right! [*She holds out her two arms toward him.*]

[53]

HALE.

Still, I must do my duty.

ALICE.

[*Her hands drop to her side.*] And what about your duty to me!

HALE.

[*Takes one of her hands, and holds it in his own.*] Could you love a coward?

ALICE.

Yes, if he were a coward for my sake.

HALE.

I don't believe you!

ALICE.

It is true, and if you love me you'll stay!

HALE.

If—*if* I love you!

ALICE.

Yes, *if* you love me! Choose! If you go on this mission, it is the end of our love! Choose! [*She draws away her hand.*]

HALE.

There can be no such choice,—it would be an insult to believe you.

ALICE.

[*In tearful, despairing entreaty.*] You heard them—it's to *death* you're going.

HALE.

Perhaps—

ALICE.

[*In a whisper.*] You *will* go?

HALE.

I must!

ALICE.

[*A wild cry.*] Then I hate you!

[54]

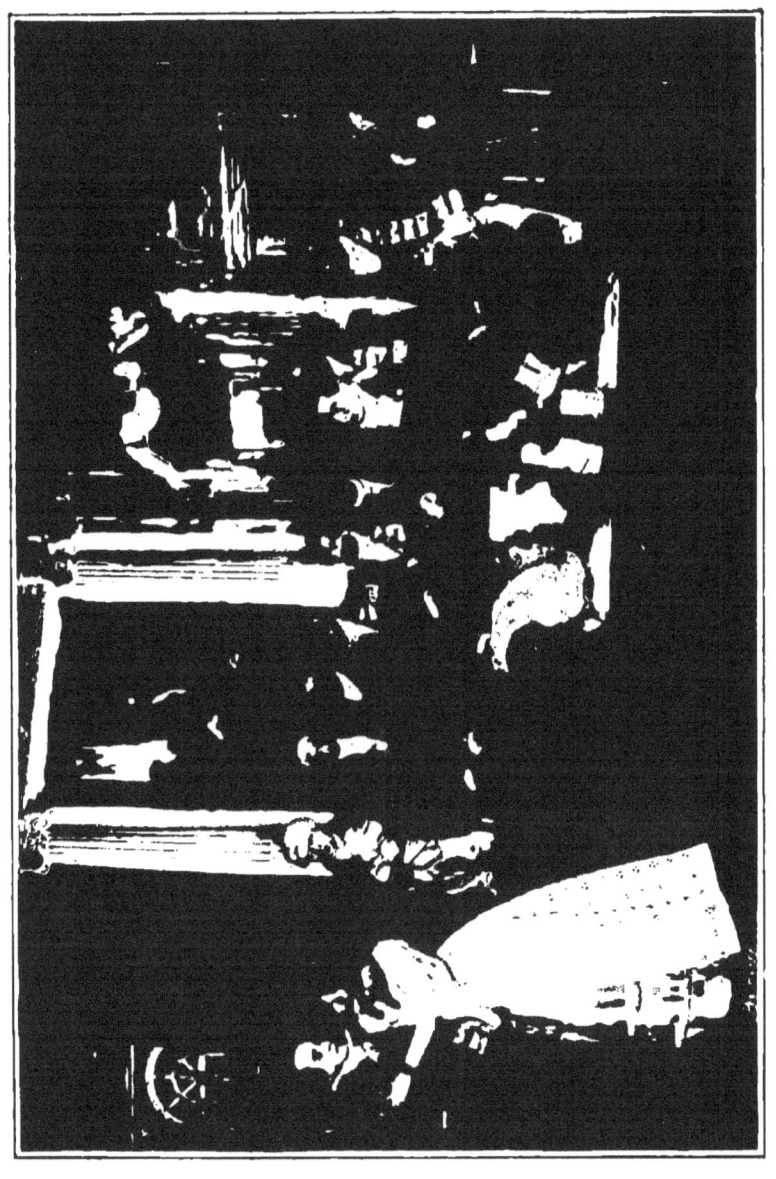

You *Will* Go?

HALE.

And I *love you*, and always will so long as a heart beats in my body. [*He wishes to embrace her.*]

ALICE.

No! [*She draws back her head, her eyes blazing, she is momentarily insane with fear and grief and love. Hale bows his head and slowly goes from the room. Alice, with a faint, heart-broken cry, sinks limply to the floor, her father hurrying to her as the Curtain Falls.*]

Act the Third

Act the Third

The First Scene

SEPTEMBER, 1776. *Long Island, opposite Norwalk. The* Widow Chichester's *Inn. Time: Night. A party of British officers and soldiers, including* Cunningham, *and also some men in civilian's dress are discovered drinking, the* Widow *serving them. At the curtain they are singing a jolly drinking song. As the* Widow *refills each mug, each soldier takes some slight liberty with her, pinches her arm, or puts his arm about her waist, or kisses her wrist, or "nips" her cheek; she takes it all good-naturedly, laughing, and sometimes slapping them, or pushing them away, and joining them in their song. At the end of the song* Fitzroy *swaggers in by the door on the right. He is greeted with shouts and cheers. The* Widow *has gone behind the bar.*

CUNNINGHAM.
[*Seated on the corner of the table, which is at the left.*] Here's a man for a toast! A toast, Major!

ALL THE SOLDIERS.
[*Rapping the table with their mugs.*] A toast! A toast!

FITZROY.
For God's sake, give me stuff to drink it in! [*Leaning with his back against the bar.*] I've a hell's thirst in my throat. [*The* Widow *is ready, as he speaks, to fill his glass across the bar. As she is filling it he kisses her roughly, and she, to elude him, moves and thus spills half the liquor; he tries to seize her, but she pushes him off.*]

WIDOW.
Enough of that! Kiss the liquor—it's your equal! [*The soldiers are laughing, singing, and filling their mugs.*]

[59]

FITZROY.

Ain't she coy, the Widow Chic! Well, boys,—here you are to our Royal Master! Long life to King George!

WIDOW AND ALL.

[*Holding up their glasses and rising.*] Long life to King George! Hip! Hip! [*All drink, and then sit down again, some of the men going on with the song.*]

FITZROY.

Here's another!

CUNNINGHAM.

Give us a wench this time!

ALL.

Yes, a wench! Give us a wench's name!

FIRST SOLDIER.

Yes, if you can't give us the wench herself, give us her name!

FITZROY.

[*By their table.*] What's the matter with the Widow for a wench? [*All laugh, including* Fitzroy, *who jeers derisively.*]

WIDOW.

[*Coming to* Fitzroy.] You're a gallant soldier to poke fun at the woman who supplies you with drink! I've been hugged many a time by *your* betters! [*A general murmur of approval from the soldiers,* "Right for the widdy!" *etc., etc.*]

FITZROY.

[*Bowing low, with mock courtesy, and taking his hat off as he bows.*] I ask pardon of your Highness! [*All guffaw. She makes a mocking bob curtsey and goes back to the bar.*]

CUNNINGHAM.

Go on with the toast, we're thirsty.

ALL.

[*Shouting and pounding on the table.*] Your toast! Your toast! [*As they shout,* Hale *enters, from the right, very quietly and goes to the bar. He is dressed in a citizen's dress of brown cloth and a broad-*

brimmed hat. No notice is taken of him except by the Widow, *who gives him a mug and a drink and watches him a little curiously through the scene.*]

FITZROY.

Here 's death to George Washington!

ALL.

Hurrah! Death to George Washington!
[Hale *has suddenly fixed his eyes on* Fitzroy, *and shows that he finds something familiar in his voice and manner, and is trying to recall him.* Hale *has, at the giving of this toast, lost control of his muscles for a moment,—lost hold of his mug, it drops, and the liquor spills.: As the others put their mugs down,* Hale *is stooping to pick up his. The noise when he dropped the mug and his following action bring him into notice. He comes forward as* Fitzroy *goes up stage.*]

CUNNINGHAM.

Hello! Who 's this?

ALL.

Hello! Hello! [Fitzroy *doesn't pay much attention; he is talking with the* Widow *at the bar.*]

HALE.

Gentlemen, I am an American, loyal to the King, but of very small account to His Majesty.

CUNNINGHAM.

[*Tipping back his chair.*] What 's your name?

HALE.

Daniel Beacon.

FIRST SOLDIER.

What 's your business here?

HALE.

I 'm a teacher, but the Americans drove me out of my school.

CUNNINGHAM.

[*Crossing behind* Hale *to the bar, where he gets another drink.*] For your loyalty, eh?

[61]

HALE.

Yes—for my loyalty.

FIRST SOLDIER.

[*Bringing his fist down hard on the table.*] The damned rebels!

HALE.

I am in hopes I can find a position of some sort over here.

WIDOW.

[*Who has been half listening.*] Can't you teach these soldiers something? Lord knows they 're ignorant enough. [*Comes out from behind the bar and places a big flagon of wine on the table. Takes away the empty flagon.*]

FIRST SOLDIER.

Widdy! Widdy! [*All laugh. Fitzroy joins them again.*]

WIDOW.

[*Behind the men at table.*] Well, have you heard what the Major here says—you drunken, lazy sots?

CUNNINGHAM.

What 's that?

FITZROY.

General Howe's new plans. [*The men lean over the table to hear.*]

CUNNINGHAM.

Are we to make a move? [*Fitzroy nods his head impressively several times. The men look at each other and nod their heads.*]

WIDOW.

[*Poking Cunningham with her elbow.*] Bad news for you, lazy! Lord! How the fellow does love the rear rank.

CUNNINGHAM.

Shut up! Let 's hear the news!

WIDOW.

You 've a nice way of speaking to ladies!

CUNNINGHAM.

[*Growls in disgust.*] Bah!

[62]

FITZROY.

It comes straight from headquarters ! [*The men gather more closely about* Fitzroy, Hale *with them, with calm, pale face, showing his suppressed excitement.* Fitzroy *continues in lower tones.*] General Howe is going to force his way up the Hudson and get to the north of New York Island. [*An instantaneous expression of fear crosses* Hale's *face.*]

CUNNINGHAM.

[*Grunts.*] Huh ! What's that for ?

WIDOW.

Ninny !

FITZROY.

Use your brains !

WIDOW.

[*Laughing.*] Use his *what?*

FITZROY.

Hush, Widow Chic ! If we can get to the north of New York Island without their being warned, we'll catch Washington and cage what is practically the whole American army ! They'll have to surrender or fight under odds they can never withstand.

FIRST SOLDIER.

Well ! What's to prevent the scheme ?

FITZROY.

Nothing, unless the Americans should be warned.

CUNNINGHAM.

If they have an inkling of it they can prevent us getting up the Hudson, eh ?

FITZROY.

Precisely. In any case if they're warned it won't be tried, because Washington wouldn't be trapped and after all Washington is the man we want to get hold of.

CUNNINGHAM.

Wring Washington's damned neck, and we won't have any more of this crying for liberty !

[63]

FITZROY.

The expedition is planned for to-morrow night, and there's practically no chance for him to be warned before then.

FIRST SOLDIER.

Have you authority for this, sir?

FITZROY.

The orders are being issued now,—it's been an open secret among the men for two days. Down at the Ferry Station the betting is this business finishes the rebellion. [*The* Widow, *in answer to a signal from one of the men, comes out from behind the bar, with another flagon of wine.*] They're giving big odds.

CUNNINGHAM.

Can't finish it too soon to please me. [*Rises unsteadily.*] Fighting's dangerous work!

WIDOW.

[*Filling his cup.*] That's a brave soldier for ye!

CUNNINGHAM.

Shut up, damn you!

WIDOW.

I'll shut when I please.

CUNNINGHAM.

You'll shut when I say! You old *hag!*

WIDOW.

"Hag!" [*Slaps his face.*]

CUNNINGHAM.

Hell! [*Throws the wine in his mug in her face. Hale, who has sprung up, knocks his mug out of his hand with a blow.*]

HALE.

You coward! [*All the soldiers show excitement. Several rise. Widow goes to the bar, wiping the wine from her face; she is crying, but soon controls herself.*]

CUNNINGHAM.

What damn business is it of yours?

Act Third

HALE.

It's every man's business to protect a woman from a brute!

CUNNINGHAM.

Hear the pretty teaching gentleman quote from his reader!

FITZROY.

[*Rises. He has noticed* Hale *for the first time.*] Who is this?

HALE.

Daniel Beacon.

CUNNINGHAM.

A teacher the Rebs have driven out of New York.

FITZROY.

[*Who has looked at* Hale *curiously, turns to the* Widow.] Have you ever seen him before?

WIDOW.

Not to my knowledge.

FITZROY.

[*At the bar with the* Widow.] There's a something about him damn familiar to me. I'm suspicious! Here you, Beacon, how do we know you're not some Rebel sneak?

ALL.

[*Rising.*] What's that?

CUNNINGHAM.

That's true enough! What's your opinions?

ALL.

Make him speak! Make him speak. [*A general movement among the soldiers.*]

FITZROY.

Yes, if you *are* a loyalist, give us a taste of your sentiments!

CUNNINGHAM.

A toast will do! Give us a toast! [Fitzroy *turns aside to the* Widow.]

ALL.

[*In a general movement, seizing* Hale *they put him on top of table.*]

Come on, give us a toast!

[65]

FITZROY.

[*To the* Widow.] I 'm suspicious of this fellow! I 've seen him somewhere before. [*He looks at* Hale *attentively, unable to recall him.*]

ALL.

Give us a rouser! There you are! Now give us something hot!

CUNNINGHAM.

A toast for the King, and then one with a wench in it.

HALE.

Here 's a health to King George! May right triumph and wrong suffer defeat!

ALL.

Hip! Hip! To the King! [*All drink except* Hale, *who only pretends, which* Fitzroy, *who is watching intently, notices.*]

FITZROY.

[*To the* Widow.] He didn't drink! I am sure of it!

WIDOW.

No! *I* think he *did!*

CUNNINGHAM.

Now for the wench!

HALE.

To the Widow Chic—God bless her. [*All laugh except* Cunningham, *who says,* "Bah!" *and ostentatiously spills his liquor on the floor.*]

HALE AND ALL.

The Widow Chic! Hip! Hip! [*All drink, and then the soldiers take* Hale *down, and all talk together, slapping each other on the back, drinking, starting another song, etc.* Hale *sits by the table.*]

FITZROY.

[*To the* Widow, *suddenly.*] By God! Now I know! [*In a voice of conviction and alarm.*]

WIDOW.

[*Frightened by his voice and manner.*] What?

FITZROY.

Who he is! He's my girl's white-livered lover, one named Hale!

WIDOW.

Are you sure?

FITZROY.

Almost,—and if I'm right, he's doing spy's work here! Get plenty of liquor; if we can drug him he may disclose himself! Anyway, we'll loosen his tongue! [Widow *exits at back, with an empty flagon.* Fitzroy *joins* Hale *and the other soldiers; as he does so,* Hale *rises; he has grown uneasy under* Fitzroy's *scrutiny.*]

HALE.

Well, gentlemen, I must retire for the night. I haven't a soldier's throat for wine.

CUNNINGHAM.

Good! So much the better—the more for us! [Hale *goes toward the door at back;* Fitzroy, *from the right, goes at the same time to meet him. They meet at the door, back.*]

FITZROY.

Still, won't you stay and have a game with us?

HALE.

I think you must excuse me.

FITZROY.

[*Angry.*] You're afraid to stay, you're afraid to drink, for fear we'll find out the truth as to who you are! [*The* Widow *comes in with more liquor, puts it on the table, and takes the empty flagon to the bar.*]

HALE.

[*Laughs.*] Oh, that's it, is it! Very well, then I'll stay! [*He sits again at the table. The soldiers start up singing "The Three Grenadiers." They all sing and drink.*]

FITZROY.

[*Interrupts them.*] Stop singing a moment! Fill up, everybody!

[67]

Nathan Hale

I have a bumper or two to give in honor of our *guest* here! [*He stands on a chair with one foot on the table, watching* Hale *closely.*] Here's to New London, Connecticut, and the schoolhouse there!

CUNNINGHAM.

Damn silly toast!

HALE.

Never you mind, it's an excuse for a drink! [*All repeat the first part of toast, but they are getting thick-tongued, and all come to grief over the word "Connecticut." Hale has answered* Fitzroy's *look without flinching, but has managed to spill his liquor. All refill their glasses, singing.*]

FITZROY.

Here's another for you. The toast of a sly wench, and a prim one, who flaunts a damned Yankee lover in my face! But I've kissed her lips already, and before I'm through with her, if she won't be my wife, by God, I'll make her my mistress. Drink to my success with the prettiest maid in the colonies! —Alice Adams!

ALL.

To Alice Adams! Hip! Hip! [*All hold up their glasses with loud cries and then drink.* Hale *again manages to spill his liquor and pretends to drink.* Fitzroy *jumps down from the chair and table to beside* Hale.]

FITZROY.

[*Loudly, fiercely to* Hale.] You didn't drink! I watched your damned throat and not a drop went down it! [*General movement of the soldiers. All rise; excitement.*]

ALL.

Show us your cup! Show us your cup! [Hale, *with a sneering laugh, holds his glass above his head and turns it upside down; it is empty.*]

CUNNINGHAM.

What's the matter with you? He knows good liquor when he tastes it! [*All laugh drunkenly; general movement again. All re-*

[68]

Act Third

take their seats, and continue singing. Hale *looks defiantly in* Fitzroy's *face, and throws his cup on the floor.*]

HALE.
Good night, gentlemen!

ALL.
[*Drunkenly.*] Good night, good night! [Hale *goes out by the door
at back, shown by the* Widow, *who exits with him, taking a can-
dle. One of the soldiers is asleep;* Cunningham *is on the floor; another under the table; they are singing in a sleepy, drunken way.*
Fitzroy *writes a letter rapidly on paper, which he finds on the corner of the bar. When he is finished,*]

CUNNINGHAM.
[*On the floor, his head and arms on the chair, whining.*] I'm
thirsty! Won't some kind person please give me a drink?

FITZROY.
[*Kicking him with his foot to make him get up.*] Get up! Get up,
I say! I have an errand for you!

CUNNINGHAM.
[*Rising, steadies himself against the chair.*] What is it?

FITZROY.
This man is a spy—

CUNNINGHAM.
Hurrah! [*Waves the arm with which he was steadying himself,
almost loses his balance.*] We'll hang him up to the first tree!

FITZROY.
Wait! We must prove it first, and I have thought of a plan.
Take a horse and ride like hell to the Ferry Station. Cross to
New York and give this letter to General Howe. He will see
that you are conducted to a Colonel Knowlton's house, with
a letter from him to a young lady who is staying there.

CUNNINGHAM.
[*Who is a little drunk, throwing back his shoulders and swagger-
ing a bit.*] A young lady! Ah, Major, you've hit on the right
man for your business this time.

[69]

FITZROY.

Don't interrupt, you drunken fool! but listen to what I am telling you. The letter will say that Captain Nathan Hale is here wounded and wishes to see his sweetheart, Alice Adams, before he dies. If you are questioned corroborate that, you understand! A young man named Hale is here wounded! That's who the fellow upstairs is, I'm very well nigh certain! The girl's in love with him, she'll come! and if it is Hale we've got here, we're likely to know it—if it isn't, well, no harm done!

CUNNINGHAM.

Very pretty! Just the kind of business I like.

FITZROY.

Your password on this side will be "Love." Are you sober enough to remember that?

CUNNINGHAM.

[*In a maudlin voice.*] "Love!" You do me an injustice, Major! [*With a half-tipsy effort at dignity.*]

FITZROY.

Mind you don't speak *my* name. You come at *General Howe's* orders.

CUNNINGHAM.

Diplomacy was always my forte. Fighting's much too common work!

FITZROY.

Go on now. There's no time to be lost! I want the girl here by daybreak, before the dog's up and off.

CUNNINGHAM.

You guarantee, Major, that the girl's pretty?

FITZROY.

[*Turning on him.*] What! None of that! She's my property! You'd better not forget that. No poaching on my preserves!

CUNNINGHAM.

[*Dogged.*] I understand, sir. [*Salutes and exits. All the soldiers are asleep. The* Widow *comes back.* Fitzroy *turns a chair to face the fire.*]

FITZROY.

Bring more liquor. [*He throws himself into the chair.*]

WIDOW.

More? at this hour?

FITZROY.

[*Loosening his neck gear.*] Yes, enough to last till morning. [*To himself.*] I warned her some day I would set to and drink myself mad for her! And the time's come! [*The stage darkens.*]

The Second Scene

OUTSIDE *the* Widow Chichester's. *Very early the next morning. The scene represents the front of the house, a low, rambling structure of gray stone, with a porch and a gabled roof, in which is the window of Fitzroy's bed-room. There is a well-sweep on the left, and a sign-post beside the road. There are trees and shrubs on each side. It is just at sunrise. As dawn begins a cock is heard crowing behind the house, answered by a second cock and by others. The sun rises and floods the scene.*

The Widow *is heard unbolting the door, and comes out on to the porch, carrying the mugs of the night before, which she has washed and which she places on a bench in the sun. A bugle call is heard, and while she is arranging the mugs, three soldiers come out from the house.*

THE THREE SOLDIERS.

[*On the porch, saluting with elaborate politeness.*] Good morning, Widow Chic.

WIDOW.

[*Imitating their salute.*] God bless you and King George! [*The*

[71]

soldiers leave porch and start off, right.] Where are you off to this early?

FIRST SOLDIER.

[*As he speaks, all three stop and turn.*] On picket duty, between here and the Ferry Station. The Major's orders. [*Fitzroy appears in the upstairs window, opening the shutters; he is without his coat; he is dishevelled and bloated; he looks as if he had not been to bed.*]

FITZROY.

Here you men! No loitering! You 've no time to lose! Remember you 're to pass no one but the girl, Alice Adams, with Cunningham. If she 's brought any one with her, man, woman, or child, don't let 'em pass.

THE THREE SOLDIERS.

[*Salute.*] Yes, sir. [*They start to go.*]

FITZROY.

Burnham!

FIRST SOLDIER.

[*Salutes.*] Yes, sir?

FITZROY.

Have you your bugle with you?

FIRST SOLDIER.

Yes, sir.

FITZROY.

Well, you change with Smith, then; take his position nearest to the Ferry, and sound a warning the moment they pass, that I may know *here* they 're coming, and be ready.

FIRST SOLDIER.

[*Salutes.*] Yes, sir.

FITZROY.

That 's all. [*The three soldiers salute and go off down the road, right. Fitzroy calls,*] Widow Chic!

WIDOW.

[*Coming down from the porch, and looking up at Fitzroy.*] Yes, Major.

FITZROY.

We're going to have some pretty sport here presently.

WIDOW.

I hope it's no harm to the young teacher who took my part last night, sir.

FITZROY.

Damme! You're sweet on him, too! He's quite a lady-killer. [*He laughs satirically and disappears from the window, leaving the shutters open.* Hale *opens the door and comes out on to the porch.*]

HALE.

Good morning, madam.

WIDOW.

[*With a curtsey.*] Good morning, sir; the Lord bless you and King George.

HALE.

Ahem! By the way, where is my horse? Has she had a good night?

WIDOW.

She's tethered right there, sir. [*Pointing off, right.*] In the bushes. It's the best I could do, having no barn. I told the boy to feed her the first thing, sir. [Hale *goes to the right as she speaks. The* Widow *stands watching him.*]

HALE.

[*Passes out of sight among the trees and bushes.*] Ah! Betsy, old girl! [*He is heard patting the horse.*] How is it, eh? Had a good night, my beauty? Hungry? Oh, no, you've had your breakfast, haven't you? [*He is heard patting her again.*] That's good! Be ready to start in a few minutes now. [*He comes back into sight.*] Will you kindly ask the boy to saddle her at once, madam?

[Fitzroy *comes out on to the porch.*]

WIDOW.

Certainly, sir. [*Goes into house.*]

FITZROY.

Good morning.

[73]

HALE.

Good morning.

FITZROY.

[*Leaning against a pillar of the porch.*] I have a pleasant surprise for you.

HALE.

[*Suspicious, walking slowly across the stage to hide his nervousness.*] That is a sufficient surprise in itself.

FITZROY.

I am expecting a visitor for you every moment now.

HALE.

[*Involuntarily stops a second and turns.*] A visitor? [*He continues walking.*]

FITZROY.

For you.

HALE.

[*More suspicious, but on his guard.*] Who?

FITZROY.

Alice Adams. [Hale *does not make any movement, but he cannot avoid an expression of mingled fear and surprise flashing across his face—it is so slight that though* Fitzroy *does see it, he cannot be sure that it is anything.* Hale *continues to walk, returning from left to right.* Fitzroy *comes down from the porch and meets* Hale *as he crosses.*] You change color.

HALE.

[*Quietly, himself again completely.*] Do I? [*Walks on toward right.*]

FITZROY.

[*Looking after him.*] Yes—Nathan Hale!

HALE.

[*Walks on with his back to* Fitzroy.] Nathan what?

FITZROY.

Nathan Hale! And you are here stealing information of our movements for the rebel army! If I can only prove it—[*He is interrupted.*]

Act Third

HALE.

[*Turning sharply.*] If!

FITZROY.

And I will prove it!

HALE.

[*Walking towards* Fitzroy, *now from right.*] Indeed ! How?

FITZROY.

If Cunningham has carried out my instructions, he has gone to Alice with a note from General Howe saying that Nathan Hale is wounded and dying here and wishes to see her! I think that will bring her readily enough—in which case we ought to hear them pass the sentinels any moment now! [*A short pause,* Fitzroy *watching for the effect on* Hale *of every word he speaks. They stand face to face.*]

HALE.

And who is Nathan Hale?

FITZROY.

A damned rebel fool the girl's sweet on. If you *are* he, and she is brought face to face with you, alive, whom she fears to find dead, she's sure to make some sign of recognition, if I know women, and that sign will cost you your life!

HALE.

It's a dastardly trick to make such use of a woman.

FITZROY.

All's fair in love and war, and this is a case of both, for I love the girl, too.

HALE.

And if I'm not—[*Hesitates.*] what's his name—[Fitzroy *sneers.*] the man you think me?

FITZROY.

Oh, well then, no harm's done. Meanwhile you needn't try to get away before she comes. I've placed pickets all about with orders who's to pass and not. [*The* Widow *comes from the house carrying a horse's saddle.*]

[75]

WIDOW.

That boy 's gone to the village; I will have to saddle your horse myself, sir. [*Going toward the right.*]

FITZROY.

[*Passing behind* Hale *to the* Widow.] I 'm hungry, Widow Chic! Is there a swallow of coffee and a bite of bread ready? I haven't time for more. [*With a meaning look toward* Hale.]

WIDOW.

Yes, in the kitchen.

FITZROY.

[*Goes on to the porch, and there turns on the steps to say to* Hale,] Don't be alarmed, I won't miss your meeting; I shall be on hand. [*Goes into the house.*]

HALE.

[*Quickly going after* Widow. *In half-lowered tones and showing suspense and suppressed excitement.*] Madam!

WIDOW.

Yes, sir?

HALE.

[*Taking her by the arm kindly.*] Dear madam, you thanked me last night for striking that dog of a soldier who had his cup raised against you—

WIDOW.

Ah, sir, it 's many a day since I 've been protected by any man, let alone a handsome young beau like you, sir. [*With a curtsey.*]

HALE.

[*Bows.*] Thank you, madam. Will you also do me a favor in return?

WIDOW.

That I will, sir.

HALE.

Then quick, leave the saddle by the horse to arrange on your return, and go a bit down the road toward the Ferry Station. Wait there! When you see Cunningham —

WIDOW.

The brute who wanted to strike me!

HALE.

Yes!—riding along with a girl, make some motion to her, wave your hand or kerchief or something. Do anything to attract her attention, if possible, without attracting his, and at the same time place your fingers on your lips—so! [*Showing her.*] You don't understand! and neither will she, perhaps. But a life is at stake, and it's a chance, and my only one—

WIDOW.

Wave my hand, and do so?

HALE.

Yes. She is the girl I love, madam, and I ask you to do this for me.

WIDOW.

And sir, I will. [Hale *starts and listens as if he heard something.*]

HALE.

Quick! Run, for the love of God, or you may be too late! [*The* Widow *hurries off, right. The saddle is heard falling in the bushes where she throws it.* Hale *shakes his head doubtfully as to the success of his plan; he goes to the right and speaks to the horse.*] Betty! Ah! Bless your heart! Be ready, old girl. I may need you soon to race away from death with! Be ready, old girl. [*During the end of this speech* Fitzroy *comes out on to the porch carrying a coffee bowl in his hand, from which he drinks. He doesn't hear* Hale's *words.*]

FITZROY.

That's a good horse of yours, Mr. Beacon. [*Drinks the coffee.* Hale *starts very slightly and turns, looks scornfully at* Fitzroy, *and crosses stage slowly.*] Our friends are late! [*He starts to drink again, but just as the bowl touches his lips, a far-off bugle call of warning is heard. Both* Hale *and* Fitzroy *start and stand still, except that very slowly the hand with the bowl sinks down from* Fitzroy's *lips, as the head very slowly lifts, his eyes wide-open, a smile of expectant triumph on his face.* Hale *is at the left,* Fitzroy *is on the porch steps, as the bugle stops.* Fitzroy *hurls away the bowl, from which some coffee is spilled and which is broken as it strikes, while he cries out,*] They 're coming! [*He comes down the steps.*]

SECOND PICKET'S VOICE.
[*Off stage, right, at a far distance.*] Who goes there?

CUNNINGHAM.
[*Far off.*] Charles Cunningham, with Miss Alice Adams, on private business.

SECOND PICKET.
Your password?

CUNNINGHAM.
"Love!" [*In a sneering voice.* Fitzroy *listens till* Cunningham's *reply is finished, then turns quickly to look at* Hale, *whose face shows nothing. The sound of the horse's hoofs is heard coming nearer and nearer. After a few seconds the third picket is heard.*]

THIRD PICKET.
[*Off stage at a distance.*] Who goes there?

CUNNINGHAM.
[*Nearer.*] Charles Cunningham, with Miss Alice Adams, on private business.

THIRD PICKET.
Your password?

CUNNINGHAM.
[*Again in a sneering voice.*] "Love!" [*The horse's hoofs are heard coming closer and then stop. There is the noise of dismounting in the bushes.*] Here! just tie these safe! Come along now, miss! [Cunningham *and* Alice *come on, right.* Alice's *eyes fall first on* Fitzroy.]

ALICE.
You here! [Fitzroy *doesn't answer, but turning his face and eyes*

to Hale *directs with his hand* Alice's *gaze in that direction, and then he quickly turns his eyes upon* Alice, *to watch her face. She very slowly follows his glance to* Hale, *rests her eyes on his a full minute without making any recognition, and then turns to* Cunningham.]

ALICE.

Where is Captain Hale? Why don't you take me to him at once?

FITZROY.

[*In a rage.*] She's been warned! Who's spoiled my plot! [*Going menacingly to* Cunningham. *At this action there is one moment when unseen,* Alice *and* Nathan's *eyes can seek each other, but only for a moment.*]

CUNNINGHAM.

Not I! It has spoiled my fun, too.

FITZROY.

[*To* Alice.] That's your lover, and you know it. I only saw him a few moments in his schoolhouse, but I can't have so bad a memory for a face as all that. [*Widow is heard singing "The Three Grenadiers" in the bushes at right, where she is tying the horses.*]

ALICE.

They told me Captain Hale was here and dying! Who played this trick on me? [*Looking blankly at* Hale *and then at* Cunningham *and* Fitzroy.]

FITZROY.

Well, *isn't* he here? [*Motioning to* Hale.]

ALICE.

[*To* Fitzroy.] It was *you*, of course! You who have forced me to this ride through the night, half dead with fear, and all for a lie! Well, mark my word, you will lose your commission for this! Rebels or no rebels, we have our rights as human beings, and General Howe is a gentleman who will be the first to punish a trick like you have played on a woman!

FITZROY.

[*Going to* Alice.] We'll see what General Howe will do when

I give into his hands a man who has been stealing information of our movements for the rebel army, who has been working for the destruction of the King's men, and I will do this yet! You 've been warned by some one! I 'll question the pickets, and if I find one of them the traitor— [*To* Hale, *crossing before* Alice.] he 'll hang ahead of you to let the devil know you 're coming. [*A look at* Hale, *then he recrosses before* Alice *to* Cunningham.] There are men picketed all about—you need not hang around unless you want to. [*Aside to* Cunningham.] I shall steal back behind the house and watch them from inside —make some excuse to go in, too. I want you ready by the door. [*He goes off, right.*]

ALICE.

[*To* Cunningham, *going toward him.*] Aren't you going to take me back?

CUNNINGHAM.

Well, not just this minute, Mistress. I 've a hankering for some breakfast, when the Widow Chic comes back. [*He crosses behind her, strolls about in earshot and out, keeping an eye on them every other moment. He goes first to the old well, at the left.*]

HALE.

[*To* Alice.] You were brought here, Mistress —?

ALICE.

[*With a curtsey.*] Adams, sir.

HALE.

Adams, to see Captain Hale? I used to know him; he taught the same school with me. [*He adds quickly in a low voice,* Cunningham *being out of hearing,*] A woman warned you?

ALICE.

[*Low, quickly.*] Yes! [*Then aloud, in a conventional voice, as* Cunningham *moves.*] I was his scholar once.

HALE.

You were?

Act Third

ALICE.

Yes, in many things, but most of all in—*love!* [*Added in an undertone. In their conversation they keep a constant lookout about them, and when they see themselves out of* Cunningham's *hearing, they drop their voices a little and speak seriously. In* Alice's *speech just now, for instance, she adds the word "love" in a voice full of emotion and sentiment, seeing* Cunningham *is for the moment out of hearing.*]

HALE.

[*Softly, lovingly.*] Alice! [Cunningham *approaches.*] You found him a good teacher? [Cunningham *goes on to the porch and opens the top part of the door; he leans on lower part, looking in; he is in earshot of the two, which they perceive.*]

ALICE.

Yes, in *love* only too proficient!

HALE.

Oh, well—that was because of course he was enamoured desperately of you!

ALICE.

[*Coquettishly.*] He pretended so!

HALE.

[*Seriously.*] And didn't you believe him?

ALICE.

Oh, I did, at first—

HALE.

[*With difficulty keeping the anxiety out of his voice.*] Only at first! [Cunningham *passes on out of hearing.*] No—no—Alice, you didn't really doubt me! [Alice *cannot answer, because the* Widow, *singing, enters at this moment, and* Cunningham *draws near again.*]

WIDOW.

[*To* Cunningham.] Well, you brute, your horses are well pastured.

[81]

CUNNINGHAM.

I give you damns for thanks! Have you food for a brave soldier in the house?

WIDOW.

No, but I 've scraps for a coward who strikes women. Come in and eat, if you wish. I don't let starve even dogs! [*Enters the house.*]

CUNNINGHAM.

Seeing you press me! [*Laughing, follows her in. Since the* Widow's *entrance,* Fitzroy *has appeared cautiously in the second story window, and leaning his arm out softly has caught hold of the shutters and bowed them shut. He watches behind them.* Alice *sits on the porch steps, pretending to be bored, and* Hale *moves about with affected nonchalance. The moment they are apparently alone on the scene, they approach each other, but cautiously.*]

HALE.

[*Anxious.*] Did this Hale prove himself unworthy of you by some cowardly action? Had you any reason to doubt his passion?

ALICE.

He broke his word to me; that made me doubt his love.

HALE.

But you are still betrothed to him?

ALICE.

Oh, no; when he broke faith, then I broke troth.

HALE.

Yet you came this journey here to see him.

ALICE.

Out of pity—they told me he was dying.

HALE.

[*Low voice.*] Are you in earnest? Was it pity, or was it love?

ALICE.

[*With a frightened look about her, ignores his question.*] I can't

[82]

imagine how they took you for the other gentleman—Captain
Hale is taller; you, I think, are short.

HALE.

[*A little sensitive.*] Short?

ALICE.

I don't want to hurt your feelings, but it's only fair to you,
sir, in this dilemma, to be frank. It may save your life.

HALE.

[*Distressed, anxious, lest she loves him no longer.*] You came to
Captain Hale then only out of pity?

ALICE.

Out of pity, yes! And now "out of pity" I hope this ruffian
will take me back.

HALE.

[*In a low voice, his passion threatening to overmaster him.*] No,
no, say it isn't true! You love me still?

ALICE.

[*In a low voice.*] Be careful, the very trees have ears!

HALE.

If they have hearts of wood they'll break to hear you! [*Leaning over her.*]

ALICE.

[*Loud voice, frightened, for fear they are being overheard.*] Let
me pass, sir!

HALE.

[*Desperate, in a low voice full of passionate love.*] No! Look!
We're alone! They're at their breakfast—you drive me mad
—only let me know the truth! You love me?

ALICE.

Yes!

HALE.

[*His pent-up passion mastering him.*] My darling! For just one
moment. [*Opening his arms, she goes into them, and as they embrace
Fitzroy throws open the shutters of his window and leaning out cries,*]

[83]

FITZROY.

I arrest you, *Nathan Hale*—

ALICE.

[*Cries out.*] My God!

FITZROY.

—In the name of the King, for a spy! [*At the moment that he has thrown open the shutters with a bang*, Cunningham *has thrown open the door below and stands on the porch levelling his musket at* Hale.]

ALICE.

[*Cries out.*] Nathan!

FITZROY.

[*Calls down to* Cunningham.] If he attempts to escape, fire. [*Climbing out of the window on to the roof of the porch, and flinging himself off by one of the pillars.*] At last! I've won! Before to-day's sun sets, you will be hanged to a tree out yonder, Nathan Hale, and the birds can come and peck out the love for her in your dead heart. For she'll be mine! [Alice *starts, frightened, with a low gasp.*]

HALE.

Yours!

FITZROY.

Mine! [*To* Alice.] You remember I told you once, sometime I'd make up my mind I'd waited long enough for you? Well, so help me God, I made up my mind to that last night! [*To* Hale.] You leave her behind! But you leave her in *my arms!* [*Seizing* Alice *in his arms and forcing her into an embrace.*]

ALICE.

You brute! [*Fighting in his arms.* Cunningham *has put his hand on* Hale's *shoulder to keep him from going to her rescue.* Hale *has shown by the movement of his eyes that he is taking in the situation, the places of every one, etc.*]

FITZROY.

Look! [*And he bends* Alice's *head back upon his shoulder to kiss her on the lips.*]

Act Third

HALE.

Blackguard! [*With a blow of his right arm he knocks* Cunning-ham *on the head, who, falling, hits his head against the pillar of the porch and is stunned. Meanwhile, the moment he has hit* Cunningham, Hale *has sprung upon* Fitzroy, *and with one hand over his mouth has bent his head back with the other until he has re-leased* Alice. Hale *then throws* Fitzroy *down, and seizing* Alice *about the waist dashes off with her to the right, where his horse is.* Fitzroy *rises and runs to* Cunningham, *kicks him to get his gun, which has fallen under him.*]

FITZROY.

[*Beside himself with rage.*] Get up! Get up! You fool! [*Horse's hoofs heard starting off.*]

THIRD PICKET'S VOICE.

[*Off stage.*] Who goes there?

FITZROY.

[*Stops, looks up, and gives a triumphant cry.*] Ah! The picket! They 're caught! They 're caught!

HALE.

Returning with Alice Adams on private business.

PICKET.

The password.

HALE.

"Love!"

FITZROY.

Damnation! Of course he heard! [*Runs off, right, yelling.*] Fire on them! Fire! for God's sake, fire!

[*A shot is heard, followed by a loud defiant laugh from* Hale, *and an echoed "Love," as the clatter of horse's hoofs dies away, and the Curtain Falls.*]

Nathan Hale

A Second Ending to the Act

It was found on performing the Play that this ending of the Act, in which Hale's pent-up passion overcame his control and made him expose himself to Fitzroy, did not, as the theatrical phrase is, "carry over the footlights." In consequence a new ending of the Act was devised, which proved to be more effective theatrically. In this second ending Jasper follows his mistress, and after Alice has failed to recognize Nathan, Fitzroy, concealed upstairs, hears the servant being stopped and questioned by the pickets. The Major orders Jasper brought into the presence of himself, Alice, and Hale, and this time his scheme is successful; for Jasper, unwarned, recognizes Hale, and from the recognition the remainder of the Act is the same.

Act the Fourth

Act the Fourth

The First Scene

Saturday night, September 21, 1776. The tent of a British officer. Above the tent is seen the deep blue sky full of stars, on each side are trees and bushes. There is every little while the noise of a company of soldiers encamped close by. Hale is seated at a table inside the tent writing letters by candle-light. Cunningham is outside the tent, on guard. Cunningham's head is plastered, where he struck it in falling when Hale felled him. Cunningham paces slowly up and down.

CUNNINGHAM.

Writing the history of your life?

HALE.

[*Writing, without looking up.*] I am writing a letter to my mother and sister.

CUNNINGHAM.

Yankees, like yourself, I presume!

HALE.

[*Still writing.*] Please God!

CUNNINGHAM.

I suppose you 're making a pretty story out of your capture!

HALE.

No, I 'm only telling the truth—that I got the best of two pretty big men, yourself and Fitzroy. [*Half smiling. This is said not at all in the spirit of boasting, but only to ridicule* Cunningham.]

CUNNINGHAM.

Yes, and don't forget to add how you were captured by the picket close to the Ferry Station.

[89]

HALE.

[*Looks up.*] Yes, because, hearing Fitzroy's cries, the picket threatened if I didn't stop he'd shoot the girl with me.

CUNNINGHAM.

It was a narrow escape for us!

HALE.

[*With a half-smile.*] But too broad for me! [*Continues his writing.*]

CUNNINGHAM.

What else are you saying?

HALE.

[*Writing.*] Oh, that I was taken before General Howe, who probably only does what he feels his duty, although he condemns me without a trial!

CUNNINGHAM.

Yes, but with plenty of evidence against you, thanks to us witnesses and the papers found in your shoes, too!

HALE.

[*Smiling a little.*] True, I walked on very slippery ground, didn't I? [*He comes out of the tent.*] However, you didn't find all the papers.

CUNNINGHAM.

[*Surprised, changes his position.*] What do you mean?

HALE.

Oh, the men were so taken up with me they didn't see my friend and confederate Hempstead, who was waiting by the Ferry Station! I don't mind telling you, now he is out of danger, the only paper that was of immediate importance—the plan of General Howe's attack on Washington and upper New York—wrapped nicely in a leather pouch, I dropped in the bushes by the roadside when I was arrested. [*He walks a few steps toward* Cunningham *and stops. He adds cunningly, trying to get information out of him,*] That's why the attempt to force the Hudson was a failure!

CUNNINGHAM.

[*On his guard.*] Oh! was there such an attempt?

HALE.

[*Goes nearer* Cunningham, *desperately anxious to know.*] Wasn't there?

CUNNINGHAM.

[*Sneers.*] Don't you wish you knew! Go on—make haste with your scribbling! [*Crosses before* Hale *to the other side.*]

HALE.

[*Reëntering the tent and taking up his letter.*] I have finished. I do not find your presence inspiring. Have you a knife?

CUNNINGHAM.

Yes.

HALE.

Will you lend it me?

CUNNINGHAM.

No! What do you want it for?

HALE.

My mother—[*His voice breaks; he turns his back to* Cunningham.] poor little woman—wants a bit of my hair. [*He controls himself.*] Lend me your knife that I may send it to her.

CUNNINGHAM.

[*Coming to* Hale.] Yes! That's a fine dodge! And have you cut your throat and cheat the gallows! [*Getting out his knife.*] I 'll cut it off for you, shall I?

HALE.

Thank you. [*Holding his head ready, and with his right hand choosing a lock.*]

CUNNINGHAM.

[*Cuts it off roughly.*] There! [*Gives it to him.*]

HALE.

[*Puts the hair in the letter; starts to fold it.*] May I have a chaplain attend me?

CUNNINGHAM.

A what?

HALE.

A minister—a preacher!

[91]

CUNNINGHAM.

No! Give me your letter if it's finished. [*Hale comes out from the tent and hands him the letter.* Cunningham *opens the letter.*]

HALE.

How dare you open that!

CUNNINGHAM.

[*Sneeringly.*] How "dare" I?

HALE.

You shall not read it!

CUNNINGHAM.

Shan't I!

HALE.

[*Coming nearer* Cunningham.] No! That letter is my good-bye to my mother, who for the sake of my country I have robbed of her "boy." It is sacred to her eyes only!

CUNNINGHAM.

Is it! [*Spreads it open to read.*]

HALE.

[*Springs toward him, his hand on the letter.*] Stop! There's the mark of one blow I've given you on your forehead now. Dare to read that letter, and I'll keep it company with another! I mean it! I'm not afraid, with death waiting for me outside in the orchard!

CUNNINGHAM.

Either I read it, or it isn't sent. Take your choice! [Hale *looks at* Cunningham *a moment, — a look of disgust.*]

HALE.

[*He drops* Cunningham's *wrist.*] Read it! [*He walks up and down as* Cunningham *reads. He goes to right; speaks to some one outside.*] Sentinel!

SENTINEL.

[*Who speaks with a strong Irish accent, outside.*] Yis surr! [*The* Sentinel *comes on.*]

HALE.

Ask the men to sing something, will you?

[92]

SENTINEL.

They haven't sung to-night purrposely, surr, fearing it would disturb you.

HALE.

Thank them for me, and say I 'd like a song ! Something gay ! [*His voice breaks on the word "gay."*]

SENTINEL.

Yis, surr, but I 'm afraid the soldiers haven't much spirits to-night. They 're regretting the woruk of sunrise, surr.

HALE.

Well—let them sing anything, only beg them sing—*till* sunrise !

SENTINEL.

Yis, surr. [Hale *turns.* Cunningham *has finished reading letter; he has grown furious as he reads. The* Sentinel *exits.*]

CUNNINGHAM.

Hell fires! Do you think I 'll let these damned heroics be read by the Americans! By our Lady! they shall never know through me they had a rebel amongst them with such a spirit. [*He tears the letter into pieces before* Hale. *The soldiers are heard singing, outside, "Drink to me only with thine eyes."*]

HALE.

You cur! Not to send a dying man's love home! [*Goes into the tent.*]

CUNNINGHAM.

I 'll make a coward of you yet, damn you !

HALE.

You mean you 'll do your best to make me seem one! God knows the worst I have to suffer is to spend my last hours with a brute like you. How can a man give his thoughts to heaven with the devil standing by and spitting in his face! [*The* Sentinel *comes on and salutes.* Cunningham *speaks with him.*]

CUNNINGHAM.

Hale, you have visitors. Will you see them ?

[93]

HALE.

Who are they?

CUNNINGHAM.

[*To the* Sentinel.] Say he refuses to see them.

HALE.

That's a lie! I haven't refused! Who are they?

CUNNINGHAM.

They come from General Howe!

HALE.

Fitzroy! I refuse to receive him.

CUNNINGHAM.

[*To the* Sentinel.] Say he refuses to receive them.

SENTINEL.

But it's not Major Fitzroy, surr; it's a lady.

HALE.

What! [*On his guard now.*]

CUNNINGHAM.

[*To the* Sentinel.] Damn you, hold your tongue!

SENTINEL.

I was told to ansurr all the prisoner's quistions, surr.

HALE.

[*To* Cunningham, *coming out of the tent.*] You'd cheat me of every comfort, would you? [*To* Sentinel.] Is the lady young or—

SENTINEL.

[*Interrupting.*] Young, surr.

HALE.

[*Under his breath, scarcely daring to believe himself or the soldier, yet hoping.*] Alice! [*To the* Sentinel.] Is she alone?

SENTINEL.

No, surr, a maid and a young man.

HALE.

[*Again under his breath.*] Tom!

SENTINEL.

[*Continues.*] The young gintleman wishes to see you for a moment fust alone.

HALE.

Quickly ! Show him in !

SENTINEL.

Yis, surr. [*He exits.*]

HALE.

[*To* Cunningham.] What a dog's heart you must have to wish to keep even this from me !

CUNNINGHAM.

Say what you like, one thing is true: I 'm here on guard, and any comfort that you have with your sweetheart must be in my presence. [*He chuckles.*] I shall be here to *share* your kisses with you. [*Goes to right and sits on the stump of a tree there. The soldiers sing "Barbara Allen." The* Sentinel *shows in* Tom Adams.]

TOM.

Nathan !

HALE.

Tom ! [*Taking his hand,* Tom *throws his arm about* Nathan's *shoulder, and burying his head sobs a boy's tears,* Nathan *comforting him, for a moment, then.*]

TOM.

Nathan, you *saved* the States !

HALE.

[*Excited.*] What do you mean ? Was there an attack made on Harlem Heights ?

TOM.

Yes !

HALE.

And Washington?—Good God, don't tell me he was captured !

TOM.

[*More excited.*] No, of course not—thanks to your information !

[95]

HALE.

[*More excited.*] Hempstead got it, then?

TOM.

Yes; after the men went off with you he searched the spot, thinking perhaps he might find something in the bushes, and he did! he came across your wallet!

HALE.

[*With joy.*] Ah!

TOM.

So, when the British tried to steal up the Hudson that night, they found us ready and waiting, — [*He takes off his hat with the manner of paying homage, of being bareheaded in* Hale's *presence.*] your name on everybody's lips, your example in their hearts!

HALE.

[*Stopping* Tom *modestly.*] And if you hadn't been warned? [*Putting his two hands on* Tom's *shoulders.*]

TOM.

It would have been the end of us, Nathan. Washington himself says so!

HALE.

[*As if to himself, dropping his hands, half turning.*] I 'm glad I shan't die for nothing.

TOM.

Nothing? Oh! Even if your mission had been a failure your example has already worked wonders—your bravery has inspired the army with new courage!

HALE.

[*Taking his arm and walking up and down with him.*] Sh! None of that. Talk to me about Alice. She is here?

TOM.

General Howe has given her permission to see you, but only for five minutes. Can you bear it? Will you bear it for her sake? [*They stop.*]

HALE.

Yes.

TOM.

[*Looking at* Cunningham.] Is this the man Cunningham? [Hale *nods.*] Alice told me about him ; we heard he was your guard, and she has General Howe's permission to choose any other soldier to take his place inside the tent. [Hale *looks at* Cunningham *with a smile.*]

CUNNINGHAM.

[*Rising. To the* Sentinel, *who is standing at one side.*] Have you such orders ?

SENTINEL.

[*Stepping forward, salutes.*] Yis, surr.

HALE.

[*To the* Sentinel.] Very well, we 'll ask *you* to stay in place of Cunningham.

SENTINEL.

Yis, surr.

TOM.

[*To* Cunningham.] Then you can take me to my sister—now, at once. [Cunningham *crosses to* Hale *and speaks to him.*]

CUNNINGHAM.

I 'll be back on the minute when your time is finished. [*He goes out with* Tom, *right.*]

SENTINEL.

[*To* Hale.] I undershtand, surr. Don't think of me a minute. I must shtay in the tint, of course, but if iver a man could git away from his body, I 'll promise you to git away from moine ! [Hale *smiles his thanks and shakes the* Sentinel's *hand. The soldiers sing the air of what is now called "Believe Me of All Those Endearing Young Charms."* Hale *stands listening for the sound of* Alice's *coming. The* Sentinel *retires to the farther corner of the tent and stands with arms folded, his back toward* Hale. Tom *comes on first, bringing* Alice. *As they come into* Hale's *presence,* Alice *glides from out of* Tom's *keeping, and her brother leaves the two together. They stand looking at each other a moment without moving, and then both make a quick movement to meet. As their*

[97]

arms touch in the commencement of their embrace, they remain in that position a few moments, looking into each other's eyes. Then they embrace, Hale *clasping her tight in his arms and pressing a long kiss upon her lips. They remain a few moments in this position, silent and immovable. Then they slowly loosen their arms — though not altogether discontinuing the embrace — until they take their first position and again gaze into each other's faces.* Alice *sways, about to fall, faint from the effort to control her emotions, and* Hale *gently leads her to the tree stump at right. He kneels beside her so that she can rest against him with her arms about his neck. After a moment, keeping her arms still tight about him,* Alice *makes several ineffectual efforts to speak, but her quivering lips refuse to form any words, and her breath comes with difficulty.* Hale *shakes his head with a sad smile, as if to say,* "No, don't try to speak. There are no words for us." *And again they embrace. At this moment, while* Alice *is clasped again tight in* Hale's *arms, the* Sentinel, *who has his watch in his hand, slowly comes out from the tent.* Tom *also reënters, but* Hale *and* Alice *are oblivious.* Tom *goes softly to them and touches* Alice *very gently on the arm, resting his hand there. She starts violently, with a hysterical drawing in of her breath, an expression of fear and horror, as she knows this is the final moment of parting.* Hale *also starts slightly, rising, and his muscles grow rigid. He clasps and kisses her once more, but only for a second. They both are unconscious of* Tom, *of everything but each other.* Tom *takes her firmly from* Hale *and leads her out, her eyes fixed upon* Hale's *eyes, their arms outstretched toward each other. After a few paces she breaks forcibly away from* Tom, *and with a wild cry of* "No! no!" *locks her hands about* Hale's *neck.* Tom *draws her away again and leads her backward from the scene, her eyes dry now and her breath coming in short, loud, horror-stricken gasps.* Hale *holds in his hand a red rose she wore on her breast, and thinking more of her than of himself, whispers, as she goes,* "Be brave! be brave!" *The light is being slowly lowered, till, as* Alice *disappears, the stage is in total darkness.*]

Act Fourth

The Second Scene

COLONEL RUTGER'S *Orchard, the next morning.
The scene is an orchard whose trees are heavy with red
and yellow fruit. The centre tree has a heavy dark branch
jutting out, which is the gallows; from this branch all the
leaves and the little branches have been chopped off; a heavy coil of
rope with a noose hangs from it, and against the trunk of the tree
leans a ladder. It is the moment before dawn, and slowly at the back
through the trees is seen a purple streak, which changes to crimson
as the sun creeps up. A dim gray haze next fills the stage, and
through this gradually breaks the rising sun. The birds begin to
wake, and suddenly there is heard the loud, deep-toned, single toll of
a bell, followed by a roll of muffled drums in the distance. Slowly
the orchard fills with murmuring, whispering people; men and
women coming up through the trees make a semicircle amongst them,
about the gallows tree, but at a good distance. The bell tolls at in-
tervals, and muffled drums are heard between the twittering and
happy songs of birds. There is the sound of musketry, of drums beating
a funeral march, which gets nearer, and finally a company of British
soldiers marches in, led by* Fitzroy, Nathan Hale *in their midst,
walking alone, his hands tied behind his back. As he comes forward
the people are absolutely silent, and a girl in the front row of the
spectators falls forward in a dead faint. She is quickly carried out
by two bystanders.* Hale *is led to the foot of the tree before the ladder. The soldiers are in double lines on either side.*

FITZROY.

[*To* Hale.] Nathan Hale, have you anything to say? We are
ready to hear your last dying speech and confession! [Hale *is
standing, looking up, his lips moving slightly, as if in prayer. He
remains in this position a moment, and then, with a sigh of relief
and rest, looks upon the sympathetic faces of the people about him,
with almost a smile on his face.*]

[99]

HALE.

I only regret that I have but one life to lose for my country !
[Fitzroy *makes a couple of steps toward him;* Hale *turns and places
one foot on the lower rung of the ladder, as the Curtain Falls.*]

The End